Resonance

and other

SCIENCE FICTION

SHORT STORIES

by Sunnil Singh

Dedicated to my loving wife and children

Resonance

Text and cover © Sunnil Singh 2016

Published by Sunnil Singh

Edited by Narishaa Singh

A CIP catalogue record for this book is available from the British library.

ISBN 978-0-9558920-1-1

Printed and bound by

www.lightningsource.com

eBook by

Contents

Resonance

Everything is energy. Sound is energy. A young girl holds the key to our future.

Resonance

Some secrets, I suspect, are never meant to be uncovered. Perhaps, that is the way of the world. A vibrational world, where vibrational frequencies define form. Sound is vibration. Our ancestors knew this truth.

Different vibrational frequencies could be synchronised. This art of resonance became their greatest science. A science of sound, a science now forgotten. Passed down the ages by word of mouth, this knowledge made man glorious in his time.

Mysterious archaeological findings from around the world, separated by thousands of years, inexplicably share the same message. Ancient civilisations once flourished on Earth rich in a science now forgotten. Some, who were pure of heart and noble in intent, wished to preserve this knowledge for future generations. The Astra Vedas were a record of this science. Men, however, are easily corrupted. They sought to use nature's gift to rule over others. Civilizations rose and fell upon this earth, as they always do. This knowledge too faded, forgotten over time. All was lost, all but one. One book remained.

~

The silence was deafening. Ariana had heard that the desert is motionless and soundless. You really have to concentrate to become aware of the desert noises. It was the most desolate and lonesome environment she had ever been in. By day, the heat was oppressive and at night, the cold was like being locked in a freezer!

Months of research, had led her to the Nubian desert in the eastern region of the Sahara Desert where she had hoped to find a megalith. Dating back thousands of years, perhaps even to the Neolithic era when these desert sands flourished with life and civilisation; the large stone promised to hold the key to finding the ancient scrolls rumoured to have the sacred mantras of Astra yoga.

She could still vividly recall the day when she presented her findings to the scientific council of India. The oval shaped room holding eminent representatives from both the scientific and industrial world. There were holographic displays in the air before the council showing megaliths of various shapes and sizes.

'These, ladies and gentlemen are megaliths from all around the world. Artefacts from the ancient Mesopotamian, Egyptian, Greek and Indian civilizations to name but a few, all separated by centuries but carrying the same message!'

This gave rise to many a raised eyebrow, as the audience examined the displays. 'They all show that there were technologies, more precisely, sound technologies in existence. The pyramids were built using acoustic levitation. Our own ancestors employed Astra yoga and could charge weapons with energy. I believe...'

'Really my dear,' interrupted the lead scientist Dr Mera. 'Are you suggesting that these, myths are real and even more ludicrous, that they were common across the ages, shared by our people with other cultures? My dear, we had advanced civilizations whilst others were still in caves. We all appreciate the theory surrounding Astra yoga but the evidence needs to be utterly convincing. I give you this though, as scientists we all love a good science fiction story!'

Pockets of laughter spilled from the assembly.

Ariana held her composure whilst trying hard to supress her anger. 'Please don't be so naive or arrogant to think that nature shared her secrets with you alone!'

'How dare you insinuate....'

'The Egyptians proved that acoustic levitation worked and there is even evidence that....'

'Enough Ariana!' commanded Dr Mera. 'We only granted you an audience here today upon the request of your father who has been a major benefactor to our community. However, I must protest. These, ur...,' she searched for the politest dismissal, 'fantasies of yours, are as absurd as your theory that there existed an ancient world grid of electromagnetic energy upon which megaliths were built and utilized by a global megalithic culture.

'But please Doctor, just hear me out!' Members of the assembly were already starting to leave. 'We have already shown that just as water molecules crystallise into snowflakes, a liquid surface established by standing waves, can be used as a liquid-based template and be dynamically reconfigured to create structures. If we could just find the Vedic incantations used to effect these manifestations, then we could unlock a force that could change the world!' Dr Mera stepped forward and placed her hands on Ariana's shoulders. 'Change the world? You sound just like your father. Ariana, please don't embarrass him like this.' The room was empty.

Ariana stared out at the desert. The events of that day did not break her, but instead spurred her rebellious spirit into motion. At 28, she already possessed her father's drive and dedication. She had the classical features of an Indian princess. Slim, with long flowing hair, she was indeed very beautiful.

Dhana Industries had kindly provided the resources for the expedition including the Vitta 3000. Vikash Dhana was the proud benefactor of his daughter's many research projects. Her acoustic engineering background, sustained her true passion- ancient technologies, particularly sound technology. Recent revelations and live demonstrations by Tibetan monks, verified that acoustic levitation did work.

Many sceptics were now converted, also believing that the ancient Egyptians used a similar technology to build the pyramids. Ariana felt-no knew, that they had only just scratched the surface. Sound could do much more and she was determined to unveil all. She looked down at the detector lying next to her. The Vitta 3000 was a leading edge innovation that was being used to find minerals and other resources lying miles below the earth's surface. The portable version of the detector itself looked like a giant virus – a spiky ball with long protruding tubes. It was rumoured that it could detect all the way to the earth's core.

Certainly more muscle than was needed for this mission, thought Ariana. The innovations and technological wizardry born out of Dhana Technologies, a subsidiary branch, would put James Bond to shame or even make Star Trek seem primitive! No wonder it had drawn the attention of many defence technology organisations from around the world, some with rather diabolical motives.

Sunrise was but moments away. The rest of her team still slept. She would soon interrupt their slumber. Tara whose name literally meant star was certainly a star in Ariana's life. Close friends from her days at university; a capable geologist despite her characteristic disorganisation. Ariana found this endearing, somewhat like a messy teenager. Then, there was Gabriel. Tall, muscular, with an almost perfectly symmetrical face - he was undeniably handsome. He was of Swedish heritage. Gabriel had joined Dhana Industries a year ago but never completely divulged all of his fields of expertise to her. Despite that, somehow she felt that she could trust him.

They had found the subterranean cavern housing the megalith and had already excavated most of the site. Today was the solar eclipse. The megalith was here and reading the inscriptions, had to be done at the precise moment when the rays of the sun first escaped the veil of the eclipse. After a hasty breakfast, they all moved over from the camp site to the excavation. The chamber lay several metres below the surface and access was only granted by an opening in the roof of the cavern.

Amir, the young Egyptian tour guide stood by the entrance to the subterranean chamber, still rather perplexed. What started out as the five-star premium King Ramses Sunrise tour, had become a prolonged and unexpected expedition. Fortunately, his clients paid handsomely in cash.

'Madam, are you sure that this is the correct site?' he pleaded once again. 'No-one ever comes this way, really!'

'Of course Amir. You worry too much. Help the others with the equipment so we can get started,' directed Ariana.

Not that another day's pay won't be welcome, she smiled internally. Amir was really a very pleasant chap and remarkably helpful. They were living on borrowed time. The excavation was illegal. The Egyptian authorities would never grant permission for such an exercise and so Ariana was depending on the cover provided by Amir Tours!

Before she descended into the cavern below, she cast a glance at the clear blue sky. The winds were calm. Locals spoke of the 'Haboob' or desert storm that approached with very little warning. The calm before the storm. For no apparent reason Ariana felt a sense of dread rise up inside of her. With her long black hair tied back, she descended the rope ladder into the chamber below.

The energized chemical glow-sticks flung around the room bathed it with an eerie green light. The rest of the team followed shortly. Gabriel released small handheld spheres that rose into the air and flew around while radiating spinning laser probes that systematically mapped out the cavern.

The megalith stood at the southern end of the cavern, towering over the other artefacts scattered around, like some ancient and benign guardian. The rest of the team began scanning the inscriptions on the megalith into the computer that now compared them to inscriptions found on other megaliths from around the world. The same patterns emerged, confirming Ariana's theory about the ancient megalithic culture. However, the Nubian megalith held one precious secret. Hidden within the puzzles of these ancient inscriptions - was the location of the Astra Veda!

For countless ages, these incantations that could summon energised weapons and manipulate objects using sound, were passed from teacher to student by word of mouth alone. This ensured that they did not fall into the wrong hands. It had always been rumoured that one renegade Rishi or spiritual scientist had recorded these mantras in secret and compiled the Astra Vedas.

It was almost time. Five minutes to go before the eclipse. The computer had deciphered the inscriptions and computed, using the patterns inherent within the coded message, the most advantageous area to lay the map.

With everyone's help, Gabriel rolled out the thin film of plastic. Ariana poured out the liquid obtained from the laboratory onto the plastic surface. Gabriel adjusted the control panel built into one end of the sheet tuning the vibrational frequencies. The surface erupted into a kaleidoscopic ocean of bubbles that settled into a three dimensional model of the Jantar Mantar monument of Jaipur in India. It replicated, with remarkable precision, the collection of nineteen architectural astronomical instruments. The huge sundial was possibly the most remarkable feature. As the last minute passed, they all cast expectant eyes at the narrow opening in the roof of the cavern. If their research was correct, then the sun's first rays following the eclipse would somehow illuminate the precise location of the Astra Veda.

Agonizing moments passed before the rays of the sun touched the sundial. The shadow from the giant sundial pointed the way.

'I know where that is!' shouted Ariana, thrilled that it had actually worked.

Outside a sand storm was rising.

Sosuke sat in deep meditation. His lean muscular body unflinching as the thin needles with their flaming ends energized his body. This art was similar to acupuncture but far older for it enabled him to release the power of his chakras. Over the years he had activated several of these energy nodes giving him almost superhuman powers. Japanese by birth, but raised by Tibetan monks, he was eventually recruited into the Brotherhood of the Void. They had cells all over the world united with a common purpose, to protect the secrets of the ancients.

He suffered his pain silently. Blind since childhood, he had turned his energy inward. Sosuke was a very lethal weapon. His masters had awakened him now, for someone had broken a sacred seal. There would be a price to pay.

They had escaped the sand storm just in time. The flight back to India was less than comfortable. Circumstances dictated that they leave in a hurry so enduring economy class on the first flight out, was a small price to pay. Thoughts of what was yet to be discovered kept them all in good spirits.

Ariana wanted to stop of first in Mumbai before heading out to Jaipur. This was where her family lived. After saying goodbye to the others and arranging to meet again in two days, she headed home. The taxi navigated the labyrinth of noisy streets and chaotic fragrances stopping outside the Dhana residence. The day guard welcomed her in.

Sunehri rushed into her arms, her long platted hair whipped around Ariana, as she entered the door. Ariana clung to her. In her embrace everything stopped. Ariana was at peace. Pure, unselfish, this was a love to be cherished. At last, she was home.

She carried Sunehri, still clinging to her neck, into the next room and sat on a couch.

'Sunehri miss you. Sunehri miss you', her little sister sobbed.

Ariana could not hold back the tears. She took her sister's face in her hands. 'I told you I would come back, didn't I? You are my darling. Ariana will take care of you.' They hugged again.

Sunehri was autistic. Only ten years old but having being diagnosed with high-functioning autism she could not live a normal life like other ten year olds. Father paid for the most extensive care but none of that would heal Sunehri. She rarely spoke to anyone except Ariana and Maya her care worker. Father seemed to be away more often than ever on business leaving the girls alone. For Ariana, leaving Sunehri to undertake the expeditions, was painful.

Ariana spent the next two days immersed in Sunehri's love. Her little sister had difficulty communicating with the world and performing even the simplest of tasks. Ironically, her acts of random genius would easily let anyone mistake her for a child prodigy.

Two years had now passed since their mother had succumbed to a brain tumor. Everyone missed her. Ariana could still vividly remember that first day when they discovered that Sunehri was a high-functioning autistic. Their mother loved solving numerous cryptic crosswords and other maths puzzles from their daily paper. Father indulged her and purchased a volume of 'unbreakable codes' just to humor her.

Ariana remembers Sunehri reading out numbers from the open pages of the discarded book. It was only later that night, when she herself looked at the solutions; after trying in vain to solve any of the problems, that she realized what Sunehri was actually doing that day. Things had never been the same from that day forward.

Deepak was glad to hear the news of Ariana's arrival.

'So you're back, are you? Have you forgotten me already? No call, not even a hologram!' he mocked through the display glass hung on the wall.

'Sorry Deeps,' she loved calling him that, 'I've been busy with Sunehri. She needs me. God how I hate to leave again so soon, but I have to see what Jaipur will reveal. Can you come over?'

'Yes of course. Don't worry, I'll take care of Sunehri and make all the arrangements for your departure. Just keep me informed on your whereabouts, will you? You leave tomorrow?' he asked.

What a blessing you are, she thought, *but you probably already know everything I've been up to since I arrived!*

Educated at the prestigious London School of Economics, he fast became Vikash Dhana's vice president and in some ways, the son that he never had. Deepak had been there when mother had passed away and so he became an integral part of the family. Ariana suspected that Father would happily give his blessing if Deepak proposed to her. She hung up and prepared to make preparations for her flight.

The car cruised in auto mode, guided by artificial intelligence. It would deliver the deadly passenger to his destination. The Brotherhood were well resourced by many affluent and undisclosed benefactors. Sosuke breathed in the fresh Canadian air. He had one last assignment to complete before he left for India. Mining operations in the Eastern region of Quebec, near the national reserve, could disturb the ancient site yet undiscovered by the world but known to the brotherhood.

The SUV pulled up in front of the cabin which served as the office.

'Your destination sir. Thank you,' came the polite voice over the car's speakers.

'Wait exactly two minutes and then sound the horn,' instructed Sosuke.

'Yes sir,' came the reply, sounding almost glad to be of assistance.

He stepped out and proceeded up the stairs leading into the cabin. The lightweight and super strong graphene alloy walking stick serving only as camouflage. Sosuke had a keen awareness of his environment.

'Can I help you mister?' the coarse voice barked at Sosuke as he entered.

The foreman was built like a tree. Three of his companions were scattered around the room. Strong musky odours and breathing, betrayed their positions. Suddenly a car horn bellowed out.

'What the heck is going on? Go check that out!'

From within his coat, Sosuke withdrew the bear claws with his other hand. The first man hit the floor with a thunderous crash, while the second charging assailant was propelled backwards through the window in an explosion of glass. A gun was withdrawn. The bullet raced for his head but was deflected by the walking stick.

'Too slow my friends,' he laughed. Two more shots rang out. His hand a blur of motion. The stick, an extension of his awareness, cut through the air ricocheting the bullets into the walls.

'Now it's my turn gentlemen.'

It was over in a second. The authorities would undoubtedly have unanswered questions about what exactly transpired, but bears were known to attack miners. Operations would be halted in light of a public outcry.

The SUV came into position as he emerged from the cabin. 'To the airport,' he directed his obedient ride.

Now, to keep the book safe and ensure that it is not uncovered, he thought.

They arrived at the site around dusk and parked some distance from the entrance. All of the tourists were gone, having spent time marveling at the ingenuity of the designers of these stone and marble structures.

The drive from Jaipur airport, in the smoldering heat, left them feeling weak and exhausted. However, new energy filled them as they prepared to retrieve the Astra Veda. Although the site offered little in the way of opportunities for theft, thus negating the need for much security, Ariana was taking no chances.

She had visited the site several times with her father, a patriot of Indian history and culture. With care, Jacob unfolded the flexible hand-held display glass. He activated it, illuminating the interior of their vehicle with a faint blue luminance. It showed the view from the spider shaped retrieval robot that was now beginning to scuttle across the ground.

Nanotechnology gifted their little helper with a cloak of invisibility. Ariana took control of the robot, guiding it around the site. It passed by the first sunken bowl shaped sundial and crept into the second. As she suspected, an out of bounds barrier blocked the spider robots advance. Mini lasers emerged from the head and made quick work of the obstruction. It proceeded into the hidden tunnel. After several minutes it was back with Ariana.

The Indian Scientific council, stored certain rare and precious artefacts from around India and the world, permanently at this site. Ariana knew the reason. Although they would not admit it, the site, like others around the world, was a store of electromagnetic energy that seemed to energize objects and even preserve the artifacts. She raised, with a pounding heart, the wooden box that she prayed held the Astra Veda. Tomorrow morning…definitely tomorrow, she would look inside.

There was a disturbance in the field. Sosuke felt it like a blow to the chest. They had found it. An incoming call. 'The Rajput Mahal,' whispered the voice in his ear. He rose and strode out of the little roadside cafe leaving behind aromatic and spicy fragrances that captivated the guests but held no sway over him. Purpose and confidence matched his every step thanks to his other super senses that concealed his blindness from people.

Back at the hotel, the team gathered around the table. No one said a word. The early morning rays fell upon the little chest, trying to pry it open.

Suddenly a crashing noise split the silence. Startled faces turned to Tara.

'Sorry!' came the hushed apology as she bent down to pick up the shattered saucer.

'Leave it now.... just don't bother. It's ok,' Ariana pulled Tara closer.

She opened the little chest. Air rushed in. The book was aged and heavy. Fragile pages cascaded over each other as she opened the book. It smelt dusty. The contents of these pages spanned thousands of years in knowledge.

Gabriel wanted to start the scanning and decoding process now but Ariana stopped him.

'Something tells me that we should wait. I would rather take it...' The hotel window flew open filling the room with warm air.

Sosuke looked up at the open window. He opened the nanorobotics module. Millions of nanomites quickly formed a bee. It began to replicate immediately. The bees moved as if to unseen instructions, their bodies glimmering in the sun.

In the distance they could see a cloud approaching! 'Shut it, shut it now!' yelled Ariana. Gabriel threw himself at the window, slamming it shut just as the cloud crashed into it. The swarm recoiled, forming a massive ball before dispersing. Single minded in intent, they looked for an opening.

Tara screamed out in terror. Ariana felt a cold chill run down her spine. She tried to move but her legs would not obey her. Gabriel yanked his suitcase out from under the bed. The incessant buzzing grew louder. He extracted the Vitta 3000 and feverishly adjusted the sonic pulse generator.

'What on Earth are you doing?' she struggled to make herself heard above the noise.

Gabriel had no time for questions. He threw a silver sphere towards the center of the room. It instantly grew into a spiral. The bees had found a way in. The first of them charged in through the keyhole as he grabbed Ariana and Tara, pulling them over the central sphere.

'Just hold on tight to each other,' he shouted, while smashing his fist into the center. There was an explosion of blue light as a swirling mass of static energy surrounded them. The protective forcefield repelled the assault as the bees bounced of the surface.

'Any second now, wait, wait...'

The Vitta 3000 emitted a supersonic blast incinerating the circuitry of the nanorobots while the three friends remained safely shielded inside the forcefield. Little metallic bodies rained down like pebbles onto the floor and furniture.

Fuming on the inside but calm and serene on the outside, Sosuke walked away. The incident had drawn too much attention already and someone outside of the Brotherhood had access to nanotechnology. *This is not over. I always get what I want - always!*

Deepak arranged for their rescue under armed escort. Mumbai would not be safe either. Within a few days Ariana and Sunehri were flown out to South Africa. Vikash Dhana owned a private game reserve located amid the breathtaking landscapes of Sabi Sands in the Kruger National Park. Their rock lodge, situated high above the reserve, had beautiful panoramic views and was carved out of the Ulusaba rock itself. Vikash entertained his VIP guests here and often concluded lucrative deals in these pleasant surroundings.

Ariana blamed herself. *Naturally there would be others seeking the book. How could I have been so naive?* She regretted. *At least we are safe here for now, until I can figure out what to do.*

She had brought the book along, fully intending to study it further. Cozy by the flame, Sunehri slept peacefully on the couch, her features illuminated by the flickering light of the wood fire.

The days passed peacefully. Excursions around the reserve rejuvenated them both. As diligently as she tried, Ariana could not decipher the text within the Astra Veda. It did not match the classical Sanskrit held on the mainframe computer back at the research laboratory.

The study door was always left open. How could Sunehri not express an interest in the object that held so much of Ariana's attention? To Sunehri's mind, the text held no mystery. Her brain unraveled its closely guarded secrets. Who knew what was to follow.

'No, you must not read from the book! Sunehri no!' she pleaded.

'But I like it Ariana. Make magic. See...see Sunehri make magic trick.' She giggled while reciting the ancient text. A faint tremor echoed across the room as the lampshade and other loose objects rose into the air and hovered like balloons on strings.

Ariana felt the blood drain from her face. *God! What have I done?*

'Stop it! Stop it now!' she yelled at her startled sister. Sunehri burst into tears. The objects fell.

The richness and complexity of the incantations were like honey to her hungry mind. There was no way of knowing how much she had digested and now retained. Sunehri could be a danger to herself and the world as she unleased a power that she did not understand.

Brain waves have a distinct vibrational frequency of their own. Some incantations must have been more closely guarded than others by our ancestors, as Ariana was soon to discover. Barbeque or braai as it was known locally, was a favorite dinner at the lodge. The diverse ensemble of foreign guests hung around making light conversation while sampling the local beer. Rich aromas drifted up from the sizzling meat.

Soft music filled the air. Some guests reacted to the music while others continued to chatter. Sunehri swayed gently to the rhythm, completely lost in the music. Ariana stood by her side. Then a few others joined in, singing, then a few more. Soon everyone swayed to the beat, their eyes glazed over.

Ariana too was spellbound. Her gentle motion brushed Sunehri aside causing her to stumble.

Sunehri opened her eyes as she caught her balance. Instantly the guests, released from their trance resumed their conversations. A shared journey that none would remember.

The baffled lodge manager played back the video footage from the security cameras for Ariana. She said nothing. She didn't have to. There was only one thing that could be done.

For better or worse, Ariana spent the next few weeks working with her sister on the book. They had to gain control. Ariana would allow the reading of a chosen section only, and then duly observe the effects.

Sunehri could levitate objects, create forcefields and manipulate water into any form that her young mind could conceive of. A particularly favorite manifestation for Sunehri, was the shower of light that she could create. It reminded her of a fireworks display. Fortunately, these sparks dispersed harmlessly into nothing.

If the stories were true, then these incantations could harness weapons. Ariana decided to stop before the latter incantations did exactly that. Destiny, however, had other plans for them.

One morning, as a warm African sun crept over the horizon, the park rangers brought in an injured Antelope. With a broken leg and a deep wound along one side of its neck, they doubted it would survive. Ariana spoke to the park ranger unaware that Sunehri had wandered over to the van. Two of the younger rangers were tending to the animal, awaiting the reserve vet. They smiled as Sunehri gently stroked the animal's neck. The animal twitched nervously. Instinctively she began to whisper. The sound elicited the required vibration. As the energy travelled through the animal at 432 Hz, molecules recombined and the healing began. The wound closed and the Antelope rose to its feet.

'Ngaka...Ngaka!' shouted the petrified Sotho park rangers. To them, only a witch could perform such an act!

Ariana turned to see the commotion. *Great, that's all we needed.*

'Of course you can't stay at the lodge any longer.' Deepak sounded deeply concerned. His holographic image unable to conceal the worry on his face. Ariana related, with some regret, the details of her experiments with the book and Sunehri. There was a long silence as he took it all in.

'You did the right thing by stopping. There is no telling what affect this might have on Sunehri. I know someone who can help. He works for us at our research facility in Rio. I think it might be best for Sunehri to see him.'

Ariana always wanted to visit Rio but never thought that it would be under such circumstances. She called Gabriel and Tara. They would meet her in Rio.

I am eternal. All things flow through me. I know no fear. I am eternal. All things flow through me. I know no fear..., Sosuke repeated his affirmations, drawing strength and resolve from them, while the rebukes from the robed Brothers, bounced off him. He had been summoned before the elders of the Brotherhood. With head bowed, he listened. He was meant for greater things. His destiny was entwined with that of the child's.

'You will go to Rio and watch over her. You will be given one final chance to prove your loyalty. Do not fail us again!

Rio was breathtaking. The giant statue of Christ atop the Corcovado Mountain was certainly one of the wonders of the world. The Dhana Neuroscience research facility was located just outside of the city centre bordering the glorious Tijuca Rainforest.

Having twice, personally experienced the devastating effects of neurological disorders in his family, Vikash did what he could to try and spare humanity from similar experiences.

Ariana and Sunehri found their accommodation more befitting a luxury five-star resort. With its tropical gardens outside and rooms complete, with high quality furnishings, including a marble finished bathroom, they loved the place! The center was run by Doctor Hans Brinkman. He was one of the worlds' leading authorities on Neuroscience.

Tara and Gabriel had already arrived and were settled in. Deepak came to meet them. Tall, handsome with a well-kept beard, he looked more like a Wall Street banker. He took them to meet Dr Hans. Perhaps, he of all people, could help Sunehri. Dr Hans had been studying brain waves his entire life.

'Everything vibrates at a particular frequency, even brain waves. Any sound produced can be made to resonate with multiples of that frequency. Once they vibrate in sympathy, we can manipulate that frequency creating a desired effect.' Explained Dr Hans.

'Yes, of course,' added Ariana,' you are referring to scientific tuning!' Dr Hans looked suitably impressed.

'Certain electromagnetic waves in the Earth's atmosphere vibrate at about 7-8Hz. Our ordinary thought waves are around 8Hz as well. We suspect that if we can get the two hemispheres of the human brain to synchronize with each other at 8Hz, it will create a maximum flow of information and potentially activate the entire brain,' elaborated the doctor.

'Now doctor, we don't want to bore the girls,' interrupted Deepak, 'All Dr Hans wants to convey, is that we can perhaps help Sunehri. If you allow her to work with the doctor, particularly on what you have discovered recently...uh...who knows where it might lead.'

With Ariana close by, Sunehri allowed them to conduct their tests. No one else could read the book, so the idea was for Sunehri to read while the team of doctors and scientists monitored her brain waves remotely.

They all reassured Ariana that this was the only way to figure out how to help Sunehri. The days that followed proved extremely tiring for Sunehri. The tests were conducted in a large vacant room. Sunehri and Ariana stood inside, while the team watched safely from behind a large transparent glass shield. Everything was being recorded. Images of her brain were displayed around the adjoining control room. Changing colours on the images highlighted areas of brain activity.

Ariana allowed Sunehri to read certain incantations. The audience were awe struck as plastic balls, chairs and even the sofa, rose into the air performing an aerial ballet around the room. On another day, a tub of water was brought in. Sunehri read softly. Ripples disturbed the surface. The clear water bubbled and formed changing geometric patterns. Gradually a watery column rose up and fanned out like molten lava. It pinched off at the base. The liquid tentacles came together in slow motion forming a floating ball.

'Incredible!' Deepak could not believe his eyes. Seeing it right before his eyes, it seemed like magic. Sosuke too was amazed, but did not show it. He had to keep his composure. Disguised as one of the support staff, he waited.

'Wonderful!' exclaimed Dr Hans. I am getting good readings. However, they are not altogether, shall I say …extensive. I need to see other areas of the brain activated. Perhaps something more, dramatic, yes?'

Upon her request, a block of quartz stone was placed in the centre of the room. Ariana turned the pages of the book. The text on these pages were boarded with what appeared to be depictions of ancient weapons.

'Sunehri tired. Go room.' Came the soft gentle voice.

'One more darling and then we can rest,' Ariana caressed here sister's head lovingly.

Sunehri read from the book. Energy coursed through her veins. Lance-like rays of blue-white light shot out from within the quartz. The girls stepped back. Gabriel did not hesitate. Instantly he opened the partition and pulled the girls into the control room.

The quartz glowed white. Rags of flame followed, engulfing the stone. An instant later there was a blinding flash as the rock exploded with a deafening blast. Fragments smashed against the glass. Terror engulfed the audience.

Sosuke smiled. *Somehow, I will possess this power.*

After that fateful day, Sunehri refused to read from the book again. Two weeks passed.

The brotherhood reflected on these events with grave concern. The child had demonstrated remarkable power. Fortunately, no one else could yet decipher the text. It could all still end with her. The world was not ready for this knowledge. Upon first learning of the manifestations from the incantations that occurred in Africa, the Brotherhood wanted to know the full potential of the Astra Mantras. Now they knew. According to ancient texts, thermonuclear weapons could be summoned. This had to end now.

Sosuke was given the final command. As fate would have it, he had found a middle path. Yes, he would deliver the child to her fated end, but not before he acquired the powers for himself. His ancient art of meditation and chakra activation would allow him to absorb her knowledge before she passed from this world, but he had to get close to her before that could happen.

Ariana and Sunehri loved walking in the tropical gardens surrounding the facility. One day they noticed a man seated on a bench under one of the garden trees. His back was to them. An enchanting song escaped his lips. Although they could not understand the words, they were mesmerized by what they saw. His walking stick, stood upright in front of him, swaying from side to side like a cobra hypnotized by a flute charmer. Outstretched hands seemed to command the stick.

'Come closer my dears,' he said 'you couldn't possible see clearly all the way from over there.'

Astounded by his remarkable perception, they came around to face him. Sunehri gazed in wonder at the blind oriental man whose lost wandering eyes seemed to search for their voices.

'Magic, you make magic!' she exclaimed in delight.

'Just a slight of the hand my dear. Don't believe everything that you see child.'

In time they became friends. Sunehri could see beyond his blindness, beyond his inadequacies. They seemed to be on the same wavelength. Ariana too liked him but remained reserved.

There was something…something not quite right-something predatory about him.

Water! It has to be near water. That was the only way for the energy to flow with optimum efficiency. Sosuke had thought this through. He would be able to synchronize with her brain at just the right time.

Ariana was always close by. She watched as the two friends stood by the water's edge. Sunehri threw pebbles into the air and laughed as the walking stick, guided by her friends' hand, sent them gliding over the water's surface.

Sosuke makes wonderful spiced tea, she thought as she yawned. *And this afternoon sun is so relaxing.* She dozed off, still sitting on the bench.

Sosuke turned around. *It worked. Now to fulfill my destiny.* He turned back to Sunehri.

From within one of his pockets, he withdrew the six yellow and white Baltic amber beads. Sosuke placed them carefully on the ground in front of Sunehri and began to chant.

'New game! Sunehri like!

Absorbed in meditation, he focused his thoughts.

'Sosuke! What on earth are you doing?' exclaimed Deepak. Startled, Sosuke spun around in the direction of the intruder.

Not now! Not when I am so close! His presence will contaminate the exchange...I won't need anyone after this anyway-I will be invincible, declared Sosuke reaching for his weapon.

'Armor!' Instantly, interlocking metal plates grew outward from Deepak's belt buckle and covered his body. The savage blow from the stick was deflected. Sosuke rushed at Deepak, slamming him into a nearby tree. He pounded savagely upon his prey, relentlessly driving him down. Blows rained down on the armor, smashing the metal plates-pulverizing them.

Sunehri reacted instinctively, her innocent mind latching onto family love in the face of cold brutality. 'No hurt Deepak. No hurt mummy and daddy friend.'

The column of water smashed down onto Sosuke like a metal fist. It knocked the air out of him.

'You stop hurting Deepak-you stop!'

The water embraced him like an affectionate mother, keeping him trapped in a floating bubble.

Frantic arms and legs beat the water as he swirled about in the aquatic tomb.

'Sunehri no. Let him go!' shouted Ariana as she stumbled to her feet. 'Let him go darling…it's all right. We're fine. Let him go.'

Sosuke had been neutralised. Deepak assured them, especially Sunehri, that they we now safe. 'Don't worry Ariana,' he told her in confidence, 'you don't need to know the details. Just rest assured that he will be dealt with.'

Ariana held Sunehri. 'I am here darling; Ariana will take care of you.'

Deepak flew them all back to Mumbai. They needed to rest and recover. Now that the threat was gone, they all felt safer. Fireworks exploded in the night sky. Searing with brilliant light and vivacious colour, they eliminated darkness from the night. Like the numerous lamps being lit, they symbolised the triumph of light over darkness, good over evil and the return of the King Ram many, many years ago. Mumbai celebrated Diwali.

Everyone gathered at the Dhana residence. Vikash Dhana cleared his diary and made this a time for family. It was a wonderful time. Everyone was happy. Deepak and Ariana had grown closer since Rio. His gallant effort to save Sunehri had reaffirmed his place in Vikash's inner circle.

Tara and Gabriel were there too. They wished her well for her future upon hearing of the plans for an engagement. They took Ariana aside later that evening.

'Where is the book now?' asked Tara.

'Back in Rio. Deepak says that Dr Hans needs it to correlate his findings on Sunehri. Why do you ask?'

Gabriel stepped forward. 'It just seems odd how it will be of any use without Sunehri. No one else can actually read the text. I don't know...ur perhaps we're just being paranoid!'

Ariana smiled. 'I know how much heart and soul we all invested in that book. It was a lifelong dream. I'm just glad that the Doctor will actually be able to help Sunehri. Good news! In a weeks' time we all fly out to Rio again. Apparently Deepak has something to show us.'

Convincing Sunehri to go was not so easy. However, Ariana knew that it would be for her own good.

'Welcome back, welcome back! How good it is too see you all again!' rejoiced the Doctor. He led them all into a chamber more reminiscent of a Buddest monastery than a laboratory. Seated on meditation seats, each within their own space were people, some Ariana recognised from her last visit.

The nearest to them sat amidst fine sand spread all around him on the ground. He read out a mantra and the sand crystallised into a bronze coloured spear, its tip crackling with an electric charge.

'Come, come this way. I have more to show you!' as he led them outside.

They were too shocked to speak. The demonstrations in the garden outside made their blood run cold. A woman stood boldly inside a translucent shimmering turquoise forcefield while heavily armed guards blasted it with rapid gunfire. She raised her hand holding a small odd shaped object. Miraculously, serpent-like projectiles manifested out of the air and flew at the guards, binding them in a deadly embrace. In another part, what appeared to be guided bullets, weaved their way around obstacles and located their targets with deadly precision.

'We figured it out, well some of it anyway. Trying to decipher the text divorced from the effects that it produced was pointless. However, thanks to the child, we could study the patterns found in the text of related effects.' He explained excitedly.

'What are you on about? This makes no sense and what has this got to do with Sunehri?' replied Ariana.

'Everything! Absolutely everything!' they turned around to see Deepak standing behind them.

'Deepak? I don't understand...' Ariana was confused and starting to grow worried.

'It's ok. Let me explain,' he comforted her. 'By studying the text of say...all the water effects and then separately the text of the fire effects and so on, we were able to isolate patterns in the text. We fed that into the computer and gradually found that we could actually read the scriptures. Isn't that great?'

'How will this help Sunehri?' Ariana wanted to know.

'Well the good Doctor just needs to study one more aspect of her brain before he can formulate a cure for her Autism. It would really help if you would cooperate darling. The final incantation has no matching patterns anywhere in the text. It is unique. The Doctor, suspects as I do, that it contains effects of a thermonuclear nature. That is why we need Sunehri this one last time. You understand of course?' Deepak was not asking!

'Complete nonsense!' said Gabriel. 'I suspected this all along. What do you hope to get out of this?

Ariana felt her world falling apart. The demonstrations had stopped. All the participants gradually drifted off. In their place were eight shadowy figures dressed in long flowing monk robes, their faces hidden from view.

'I spent years cowering at his feet. Your father! The great man! I learnt all that I could and gained his trust and yours too, my dear!' Ariana felt light headed. She clung to Sunehri.

'I wasn't born with a silver spoon in my mouth. My parents labored and gave their blood to rich families like yours. They died never knowing how successful their son had become. The billions that I will make from this enterprise will be my legacy.' He nodded to the mysterious figures.

'These are my brothers. I managed to convince the high council that they would all be better served by enriching the brotherhood. They wanted Sunehri dead.' He laughed. 'Sosuke provided me with an ideal opportunity to gain your trust while protecting my most precious asset. Really I would never have been able to overcome Sosuke without Sunehri's help.

'Brotherhood of the Void. I know of them,' said Gabriel, 'but they must cherish these ancient treasures. Keeping them from the world is sacred to them.'

'Right you are my man! Oh, I still managed to do just that. We created tuning modules that can produce specific effects. The incantations are translated to frequency generators within each unit. Only we know the original incantations that can illicit the required sound. No, they can't be replicated either! This way we can make a fortune but still keep the science to ourselves! Now, enough talk. Ariana if you will accompany me with Sunehri this way, I am sure we can come to a perfectly reasonable solution.'

'Ariana. I stay with you. Me stay Ariana'

'Sunehri,' Ariana knelt down beside her sister, 'look at me. Into my eyes, look at me!' she held Sunehri by the shoulders. 'They want to hurt us.

Do you understand? They want to hurt us. Help me, Sunehri help Ariana please.'

'Ariana what are you doing?' pleaded Deepak, 'Don't be stupid.' The monks raised their tuning modules.

'Stooop!' yelled Sunehri, holding her hands to her ears. Sunehri had internalised the incantations. After all this time she did not need to speak the words, just think it and it would work. Everything froze. Time literally stood still. Living statues adorned the garden. She plucked a flower from a tree. The delicate petals solidified into razor sharp blades. The rotating blossom rose from her hand as it spun ever faster. The disk smashed through the tuning modules.

The world returned to normal. Ariana looked around shocked. 'Now for the book and all the copies. Burn everything Sunehri - everything.'

What was lost and now was found, returned to eternal safe keeping. The book burned as it lay in the impenetrable safe. Every printed trace of the incantations were summoned by the source and burned as well. Deepak was gone. He had escaped with a digital master disk. Ariana knew that he had to be stopped.

'If I can get the master disk, I can use it to infiltrate the central database,' said Gabriel thoughtfully, 'perhaps I can download a computer virus that could eliminate all digital copies of the book no matter where Deepak may have stored them.'

'We have to find Deepak.' There was panic in her voice as Ariana looked around. She turned to Sunehri. 'Magic, make flying magic Sunehri.'

Sunehri focused her thoughts once again. There was a terrible rumble from deep within the Earth. No one spoke, unable to comprehend what was happening. Then the vibrations grew stronger as cracks appeared in the ground. They were all lifted into the air as the ground broke free with them upon it. Like Aladdin on his flying carpet, they soared through the air.

In the distance below, Tara was the first to spot Deepak speeding way from the complex in his sleek speedster along the dusty backroad. Within seconds they were ahead of him and came down directly in front, forcing him to stop. They stepped off the 'magic carpet' and moved towards the vehicle. Deepak was waiting for them next to the speedster.

'You can't have it,' he shouted. The resources of Dhana industries were at his disposal. He touched his wristwatch which instantly activated a forcefield. Sunehri created a storm of branches, stones and other flying debris that smashed into the shield. Nothing could penetrate the shield. Gabriel stepped forward. 'No!' cried Ariana.

He placed his hand lightly on the shield and pushed forward gently. The hand went through! Deepak was caught off-guard, never expecting anyone to know the one flaw that all forcefields possessed. Gabriel grabbed the master disk from Deepak but before he could withdraw his hand, Deepak grabbed his wrist scratching the skin. He laughed sadistically. 'That will cost you angel boy. The nanobots aren't so forgiving.' Gabriel dropped the disk as the microscopic agents of death spread through his body like wildfire, destroying every internal organ. He fell.

Ariana screamed. Sunehri started to cry, eyes not leaving Deepak. The horror of Gabriel's death was finally more than her innocent little heart could take. All that emotion triggered the synchronization of the two hemispheres of her brain. All stored potential was unlocked. Even as he mocked them, Deepak knew that it was over.

Brilliant white light emanated from within the forcefield, as Deepak became a shower of incredibly beautiful sparks that flickered and danced in the open air and then- gone! The energy flowed through her, healing her, liberating her. Sunehri held Ariana. 'I am her darling. Sunehri will take care of you.'

All knowledge was lost. All but one. One little girl remained. Back home, they held each other, safe and sound. Neither knew what the future held. They only knew that they would be okay. After all they had each other.

The End

Eden Park

Imagination meets innovation
at a theme park where genetic
engineering is the main
attraction.

Eden Park

Genes, they define who we are. No two of us are the same. This diversity, is perhaps nature's greatest gift to us. As children of the universe we are fated to inherit wisdom-that is certain. What is not certain, is how we will choose to use that gift.

For ages, man has dreamt of possessing the unique gifts of his animal brothers and sisters. It is not surprising then that we applied the sacred knowledge of life to realise our dreams.

Yes, creators must create, but are we playing God in creating new species or changing our own genetic makeup? What rights should new intelligent species have, if any? The mirror of morality compels us to reflect upon which broad or narrow definition we embrace, of what it means to be human. Issues of morality and ethics continue to be debated while commercial enterprise wastes no time on such deliberation. In time all things come full circle.

~

'Jake! Lin! Rise and shine,' shouted mother from the kitchen below.

They were already up. This was one morning when mother would not need to stress about being on time. The children had been anticipating this day for weeks. Summer vacation and Dad had kept his word. Eden Park! Everyone at school had already visited or were planning to. At sixteen, he was largely independent- Lin was not. Being six, afforded her many privileges. Enlisting her brother's support was one of them. Mum insisted that he help her every morning. Jake assumed it was some misguided attempt to help them bond. Lin was adopted. Jake never understood the need for Lin coming into his home. Time, mother said, would make everything okay.

Breakfast was ready. The children gobbled the cereal with speed that alarmed their mother. Roger smiled at his children.

'Really Roger! Don't encourage them. You'll choke. Now slow down. I promise you that we'll be there on time,' reassured Claire. Shortly the family were off on their summer adventure.

The entrance to Eden Park was an invitation to magic and discovery. Marble figures of DNA helix strands adorned either side of the entrance, glittering in the morning sun. The long drive lined with palm trees ended in a grand circular path around an enormous statue of a man that the children did not recognise.

The family disembarked and waited at the entrance while Roger parked the car. He joined them shortly as they were led in with other visitors on the initial tour.

'Welcome to Eden Park,' greeted their host. The tour guide was a young attractive university graduate. All the key employees were graduates. The park brochure made no secret of this. She led them into the dome shaped building.

'First on our tour is the Innovation Centre, where technology meets imagination,' theatrically announced the proud guide.

The children gazed around in awe at the numerous transparent interactive display screens suspended strategically around the circular room. More captivating were the 3D holographic exhibits of amazing animals mimicking their real-life counterparts.

'Wow, that's amazing,' said Lin as she excitedly played with a display screen.

Sebastian smiled as the visitors moved around the Innovation Centre. Parents tugged on excited and curious children trying to escape the guided tour, preferring instead to explore unrestrained. He was headed for the age restricted attractions found on the other side of the Innovation Centre.

'Genetic engineering has opened up a world of opportunities for mankind. From stem cells and genetically engineered animals to our own pioneering work on human-animal hybrids. Many diseases that have plagued humans for generations are now a thing of the past. Thanks to the work of the eminent Dr Stephen Cann, stable human-animal hybrids are now possible. Unique enzymes amongst other discoveries are gifted by these hybrids, providing the pharmaceutical and medical industries with numerous solutions,' she said.

Gifted! How generous! He thought cynically.

Astonished faces greeted the 3D holographic presentation at the centre of the room. Animal hybrids of unimaginable beauty and splendour were being showcased. Tropical bird-monkey hybrids displayed their stuff with agility and flamboyance. A leopard paced on webbed feet as it exhibited the savvy camouflage possible from a grey countershaded body that could change colours to adapt between an amphibious and a terrestrial existence. The show rolled on.

Shortly, the tour moved outside to the first attraction. A petting zoo with a difference! Weary parents watched as their delighted children rode the unique creations. The excitable but harmless reptilian-ponies scampered around on clawed feet with their delighted passengers. Their cute adorable pony faces being the only redeeming quality as they nuzzled outstretched spectator hands.

'The primary animal acts as the base genome. Specific traits from other species are isolated and genetically engineered into the host embryo,' continued the tour guide. 'The possibilities are endless.' Detailed scientific explanations were lost on an audience whose attention was stolen by the attraction.

Sebastian continued past a host of stalls offering a variety of souvenirs, take ways, attraction tickets and other items. He paused briefly at the entrance to Fabled Wilderness.

Still enough time before Evolution, he thought. 'Strictly no admittance to anyone under 16 years of age,' warned the poster. Naturally these exhibits were designed to showcase some of the more fearful hybrids. The first enclosure had a welcoming tropical atmosphere. A waterfall thundered down, cooling onlookers with a gentle spray. Impatient visitors waited with poised cameras behind tall steel bars, hoping to catch a glimpse of the gator-lion. Their patience was rewarded as the muscular armoured body emerged from behind the waterfall. It paused briefly at the water's edge. The ferocious eyes seemed to lock onto Sebastian. A chill ran down his spine! Unexpectedly, a majestic leathery mane fanned out as the gator-lion emitted a low shrieking cry. With an explosion of energy, the four powerful legs propelled it into the air before a seamless dive into the water. Exhilarated and a little shaken, Sebastian visited a few more enclosures before setting off once again.

Evolution, one of the most popular attractions, sat on the Eastern most end of the park, bordering an immense woodland that ran down to Sanguine Bay. Dave had been to Eden Park a few times, and promised that this was the ultimate thrill. At 29, Sebastian was already a successful hedge fund investor. Taking risks provided the rush and mental focus needed to hone his competitive edge in business. Evolution promised just that. He could literally release the animal from inside himself!

The building resembled an office block rather than a theme park attraction. Large, reflective silver panels adorned the outside. Inside, there were a few other guests waiting to be taken through. The receptionist greeted him warmly.

'Welcome to Evolution. Can I take your name please sir?' he inquired.

'Sebastian Wright. I booked the Platinum Package.' A few heads turned.

'Yes of course. Just a moment sir.' Within minutes Sebastian was led away to begin his induction within a private chamber. He settled back comfortably into the reclining seat as the 3D presentation began. Without being too intrusive, a smartly dressed attendant took his blood pressure while another prepared a heart monitor. Tranquil music filled the air. The holographic presenter began.

He looks just like Michael Dwain, my tenth grade biology teacher! Sebastian smiled.

'Here at Evolution we pride ourselves on being able to bring you the richest of experiences. From localised body metamorphosis to complete anatomical evolution. Why settle for just the eyes of an eagle or the muscular dexterity of a cat in your limbs? In choosing the Platinum package, you have discerningly chosen to live without restriction!'

The pre-metamorphosis medical was complete. He was alone.

'Your full body metamorphosis will begin shortly. Remember to choose two secondary traits in addition to your primary genome. A mild sedative will be administered into your blood stream to make the transformation more comfortable. The genetic coding will begin shortly thereafter. There will be no recollection of the metamorphosis, but you will awaken refreshed within your designated terrain, that has been specially chosen to suit your new body. Due to regulations, all full body metamorphisms are restricted to three hours. Upon the final hour you will begin to feel sleepy at which time you must make your way to any of the designated rest areas.'

Great, so what happens if I refuse to sleep? Thought Sebastian defiantly.

'We will be monitoring you remotely at all times so please relax and enjoy a supreme awakening!

Finally, if you could kindly sign the disclaimer next to your seat, we will begin.'

The family arrived at Little Creek Wilds, a very popular attraction where guests could see some of the parks hybrids in a natural setting. Roger passed the tickets to the attendant as Jake and Lin settled into the Magnetron capsule. The transparent saucer shaped transport hovered a few feet above the ground and afforded the passengers unrestricted views. Magnetic levitation was achieved using the equilibrium between the craft's own magnetics fields and that of the earth's. This allowed the vehicle to roam freely without the need for guide rails.

Roger reassured Claire. 'They'll be perfectly fine. Don't worry. Anyway, Jake will take care and it's programmed to go really slow.'

The children waited eagerly for the attendant to give the all clear. 'You're good to go!' he said. Jake eased the Magnetron forward.

Sebastian awoke slightly disorientated. However, within seconds he was drinking in the feedback from his heightened senses. Intoxicating! The earthy smell of the forest floor rushed up to greet him as did the salty tang of the ocean miles away! Even the soft murmur of the leaves felt heavy in his ears. A leopard. That was his base genome. To enhance the experience, he had chosen wolf-like perception and an aquatic adaptation. The extra limbs were a bonus on the platinum package!

Tough leathery skin covered him. The six slender powerful limbs awaited his command. The cooling sensation of escaping air, on either side of his neck, verified the presence of gills. His entire torso quivered with energy, locked like coiled springs within his muscles.

Shards of light pierced through the forest canopy. He was alone. *Time to see what this baby can do!*

Looking up, Lin and Jake were transfixed by the myriad of fluttering leaves that danced above their heads. Further ahead splashes of water from a stream, cascaded over tiny waterfalls. The scene that greeted them was enchanting. They were calmed, almost hypnotised, by the eyes staring back down at them. The bird-monkeys were acrobatic aerial dances second to none. Their flamboyant, winged arms grasping branches as they soared though the air, creating a gloriously resplendent show. A family of penguin-ducks hurried into the water as the Magnetron passed by. Minutes felt like hours as the two explored. Occasionally they passed other visitors who waved at the pair from within their transparent carriages. The sun was gradually dipping behind the horizon. Threads of light lingered in the sky as Jake emerged onto a grassland.

Lin was anxious to get back. The control panel issued a reminder for returning. 'I want to go back. I'm scared', she pleaded.

'Oh, grow up! It's not that late! If we are overdue, base will automatically navigate us back. We still haven't seen everything that I wanted to see. I don't always have to do what you want!' Lin fought back the tears. Huge African Buffalo-Elephants grazed in the distance. Their formidable curved horns a prominent warning to any enemies. Overhead two ranger Magnetrons sped by.

The control panel came to life. 'All park rides are now closed. Please return to your point of origin. All magnetrons will revert to automatic control within fifteen minutes.'

'Something's wrong,' cried Lin, 'please take me back!'

Great, what a waste, thought Jake as he decided to turn back. Startled by the speeding ranger

Magnetrons, the Buffalo-Elephants panicked. The stampede roared across the field.

'My God, they're heading straight for us!' shouted Jake.

Sebastian bolted through the woods, weaving between trees and bounding oven fallen branches. The assault on his senses was electrifying. He'd never felt so alive! Acute hearing detected a disturbance in the air overhead. Sebastian paused. Machines in the distance. Searching, searching for something on the ground. Entwined with this came the subtle but undeniable echo of the recall to a rest area. Sebastian ignored it!

I'm having too much fun. They can wait. Not even sleepy yet.

Presently he came to the perimeter of his enclosure. Steel fencing stretched in both directions. He ran alongside it for a while. Something up ahead caught his eye. The mangled fence was an open invitation to Sebastian. Something incredibly strong had torn through it. He could not resist exploring what lay on the other side any more then he could resist speculating with his investor's wealth on high risk ventures. As he passed through the opening, dense vegetation enfolded him.

Another terrain, possibly someone else's designated area, speculated Sebastian.

Instantly his newfound predatory senses went on alert. Something menacing approached. Whatever it was, it was trying to escape its aerial pursuers. Collision seemed inevitable. Without a seconds delay he leapt forward. His pounding heart echoed his racing feet. Relief swept over him as he cleared the dense enclosure and broke free onto an open field.

What on earth...? he shuddered.

Preoccupied with getting clear of the unknown danger, he was unable to utilise his new abilities efficiently and detect the chaos ahead. He braked abruptly, just avoiding being trampled by the herd. The stampeding animals rushed past. Despite their panicked state they reacted immediately to the presence of a predator-even a small one! They turned in unison like a flock of birds avoiding the threat.

Lin clung to Jake terrified. He tried to veer to the right hoping to avoid the wave of charging feet. The Magnetron was slow- infuriatingly slow! He closed his eyes. The noise was deafening and the magnetron rocked in air currents created by the stampede.

We're still alive. But how? Wondered Jake. As they changed direction, a Buffalo-Elephant on the fringes of the herd, caught the sluggish magnetron knocking it violently aside.

Sebastian saw the magnetron crash into the bushes and disappear from sight. Only a cloud of dirt and grass remained of the herd as they dwindled into the distance. He raced to the point where the magnetron had disappeared. Nothing. He dove gracefully into the dense growth.

Well here goes nothing. This certainly is turning out to be a grand day, and where are the rangers? Aren't they watching me remotely?

The light of day drained away as the sun sank lower in the sky, giving way to the velvety dark of night. In the dark forest his senses heightened. His human mind, however, nurtured a sense of claustrophobia with the confining darkness. He pressed on.

The magnetron came to an abrupt stop. Lin was crying. Jake comforted her in his arms, grateful that she was unharmed. After all, she was his sister. Faced with danger, he felt an unfamiliar sense of responsibility for her. He tried to open the door and then hesitated. Something moved outside. Slivers of moonlight spilled through the dense canopy of vegetation revealing lemon-yellow eyes staring back at them. Jake froze in terror. He instantly turned Lin into his body trying to shield her from the fearful sight. Razor talons screeched against the magnetrons frame. From something unseen, tentacles sploshed against the glass. Jake couldn't believe his eyes. The adrenalin flew through his veins but he couldn't move a single muscle, not even to scream. The absolute horror completely paralyzed him.

The six shadowy figures circled the magnetron as Sebastian drew close, his superb night vision allowing him to see from a distance, without compromising his presence. Two terrified children cringed within the stranded craft. Abandoning any sense of self-preservation-most uncharacteristic of himself, Sebastian charged.

He slammed into the nearest and smallest of the party and recoiled violently from the impact. It felt like hitting a brick wall. His own talons useless against the armoured shell.

This isn't going to work! Maybe I can lead them away, he thought.

Sebastian broke through the dense growth. His six feet pounding the ground hard as he tried to distance himself from his pursuers. This clearing lasted only a few metres and another dense overgrowth was fast approaching. He was exposed. A fleeting glance confirmed what his heightened senses already knew- they were onto him. Blood rushed into his pounding heart as he sped towards cover. *What a mistake,* he thought. From the moment that Dave had first suggested it, Sebastian harboured reservations. *Well, too late for that now,* he regretted. Alone and on the run. Survival was entirely up to him. *No rock climbing companion this time!*

Water! He could almost feel it. Somewhere up ahead was an aquatic retreat. Branches slammed into his face as he dove into the overgrowth. He was guided now more by his other heightened senses than sight. Despite the dense growth he quickened the pace. Limbs burned. *Yes!* Sebastian dove in. Water welcomed him as his gills opened. Choosing a multi-terrain adaptation was brilliant. The eyes adjusted, as a second, but transparent pair of eyelids moved down. *Made it!* He moved ferociously through the water. His undulating body cutting forward. Something moved ahead. In an instant it descended onto him. First just a shadow blocking out the surface moonlight- then a chocking embrace. Pain seared through his body as the bite released its venom. Total darkness followed.

The search party found the children safe but petrified. Tucked away safely into another carriage, they were soon reunited with their parents. Lin still clung to Jake who shouldered his new responsibility with approving glances from his parents. Roger was grateful for the safe return of his children but still fuming at what he referred to as blatant irresponsibility by the park, in allowing such a calamity to even occur.

'You understand of course sir, that this must be kept entirely confidential,' said the Park Manager. 'We don't want to spread panic over an isolated incident or tarnish the image of the park. The trustees have granted me full authority to make any compensation that you deem necessary. We deeply regret the entire incident and ask only that you and your family sign a Confidentiality Agreement, whereupon I will process the compensation.'

Well, I suppose they should pay for what happened to my family. Seems only right. 'Fine, but I must tell you that I don't like this one bit.

However, if it's in the best interest of all- then so be it.'

Consciousness swept over him like rivers of molten lava as the venom gradually retreated from his blood. Pain seared through this brain as he tried to discern the muffled voices around him.

'You should have let him die. He'll lead them straight to the den you know.'

'Nonsense! They can't track him anymore-my bite saw to that as well.'

'Wonder woman, wonder woman or should I say Hydra of the Deep.'

'Plug it shorty or else I'll…'

'Enough! He's awake.

Sebastian tried to move but the restraining vines hugged him tightly. He blinked profusely as he tried to make out the strange assembly.

'Greetings leopard boy. So what brings you to our neck of the woods? Sightseeing?' came the mocking voice. Sebastian looked up at the gigantic frame of a bear-man and tried to speak. Only a rasping yowl escaped his lips.

'Nope, don't try to speak mate, you can't, not yet anyway,' came the sober response of the turtle hybrid. 'Anyway, what's with whacking me and all? We weren't aiming to hurt the kids you know, just get them out of there you know. Easy bro!'

'Let me introduce you,' said the bear-man. 'I am Marcus. Leader of this forgotten and desolate bunch of misfits whom I utterly love to bits! This charming fellow is Denzel. He's got more guts than brains and an armoured shell to match as you discovered tonight.'

'Hey!'

'This beauty is Celestra. She rendered you unconscious and also revived you tonight. Miracle isn't it!' Marcus sounded like a proud father.

With her fangs and forked tongue hidden from view, she was remarkably beautiful and could pass for human; that is if you didn't notice her flamboyant scaled back with its deep hues of red and blue!

'Believe us, there's more to her bite then meets the eye. Now the rest of the crew you will get to know later-if they let you.' Something chuckled in the corner of the den.

'It's decision time for you mate. In a short while, depending on when you first transformed, the metamorphosis will become permanent,' continued Marcus. 'A little known fact. That's not in the brochure for the platinum package is it mate? So, you can choose to remain a little kitty cat and scamper around on all six, or you can choose to be like most of us- human with certain residual gifts from our alter egos. Just nod your head once for option one or twice for option two.'

Again that annoying chuckle reverberated through the den. Sebastian nodded twice. Celestra leaned forward and administered a gentle bite on the upper part of his neck. Sebastian passed out again.

When he came around he could feel his hands and face again. Two powerful limbs remained as did his gills and protracted teeth.

'Well, well-not bad,' remarked Marcus, 'You can never tell how the regression will go!'

Sebastian could speak. 'Who are you all?' he asked drained and confused.

'We're the forgotten ones,' replied the eerie green and blue hybrid. His tentacles flapping in the air wildly as the changing colours of his translucent body revealed his failure to hide his emotion. 'Hell, not really. He knows we're out here. Mistakes, failures – call us what you want. Testimony to his imperfection!'

Stephen Cann! They're talking about the founder of human hybrid engineering.

Marcus elaborated. 'Fully body metamorphisms might be entertaining but have little practical use, unless you want to eat your enemy!'

'I don't follow,' remarked Sebastian honestly.

'The military, you idiot!' barked another annoyed hybrid. 'Where do you think he gets his millions from?'

'Only human hybrids can manipulate machines effectively while still maintaining biological supremacy. However, not all combinations prove useful. That's how the first of us ended up here. It was only after Celestra joined our family that we could convert fully transformed hybrids like yourself. They released her too quickly, long before her unique abilities were fully developed and realised. Her 'love bite' as we affectionately call it, has the potential to partially reverse the transformation. Works wonders-usually. Some prefer to remain in complete metamorphism while others struggle with the reality.' Marcus turned away.

'That's what became of Ike,' interjected Celestra, 'Marcus' son. He psychologically couldn't handle it at his age. Drove him insane. We suspect that they were looking for him tonight. That is why we were out there, hoping to find him first. You could help you know. I suspect that you have the most acute senses of any of us. That is why I let you live. So what will it be, will you help us?'

Sebastian strode forward and stood at the mouth of the den. Moonlight painted a silver streak across the ocean below but not so bright as to dull the stars that speckled and glittered in the heavens above. For the first time he felt a kind of peace settle over him that his hectic and self-absorbed life had previously denied him. 'Well, now that you mention it, I have no other pressing engagements.'

In the days that followed, Sebastian led several teams of hybrids in search of Ike. His super senses locking onto the boy several times but only to lose him again. Ike was unlike any other hybrid Sebastian was told. He was a combination of several animals with the ability to camouflage. The cash strapped Marcus had turned to Dr Cann in desperation when Ike had been diagnosed with cancer. In return for his son's treatment Marcus volunteered for the Genesis program- human hybrid engineering.

Human hybrid engineering was still in its infancy. The procedure saved the boy but transformed him into an abomination. His young mind could not handle the trauma of body metamorphosis. Dr Cann had insisted that it was a freak accident. Marcus harboured a deep suspicion about the true intent of Dr Cann.

Rain beat down ferociously that day when they finally found Ike; curled up and shivering in the dark corner of a cave just north of Sanguine Bay. His body was dying, which explained why they were finally able to track him. Fortune smiled on Marcus. He had managed to reach Ike before the company could reclaim the prize that had managed to elude capture for years.

It took Celestra three days to nurture Ike's body back to health. His mind was not so easily persuaded. Only a father's undying affection and warmth could do that. Watching his son's ordeal only ignited a hatred that should have died with the boy's salvation.

'Sorry Ike. We know that you took care of us but this is just suicide. Please understand,' implored the aged Arvina. Her four deformed arms marred the beauty of her human torso with bird-like head; Dr Cann's attempt to create his own version of the divine mythical Buddhist creature, Karura. 'What good would I be anyway?' Marcus hugged her affectionately before she left with a small group of hybrids.

'We deserve the truth. By God, we've earned the right to it!' declared Marcus. 'For too long he has hidden his shameful truth from the world. Who's with me?' The den exploded with a chorus of yelps, shrieks, whistles, hisses and other indistinguishable calls of solidarity.

The morning sunrise was a breath-taking display of radiant colour. Even the dew drops, adorning the forest, seemed to glow with their own golden radiance. The soft rays that should have brought warmth to a new day, only acted to solidify the reality of their predicament. Sebastian rested on an enormous branch of a tree overlooking a deep ravine. He tried to gather his thoughts that were fragmented with the ominous certainty of impending suffering. The unlikely band of hybrid soldiers specially chosen by Marcus and Sebastian would led the morning assault on Eden Towers; the office and home of Dr Stephen Cann. Marcus knew that Ike would have to accompany them. No one else would be able to penetrate the tower block undetected. He would not lose him again! Sebastian would lead the assault from the eastern side once Ike and a few other hybrids disabled the control hub situated underground.

Ike was the first in. Surveillance cameras were deceived by the camouflaged intruder. Thermoregulation and antifreeze-like blood rendered the thermal detectors useless. An accomplice issued a sonic echo to alert Sebastian. Eden Towers relied heavily on its technology for protection; a grievous mistake easily manipulated by the hybrids. Eden Park needed to maintain the farce of being just a theme park attraction, so the few security details present, were easily dispatched by the hybrids.

Denzel insisted on going along despite the protest from the other hybrids. Sebastian recalled the discussion with amusing clarity.

'Marcus, you can't be serious. He's got the thing. You know what I mean. They'll know we're coming from miles away!' Denzel was the result of blending sea turtles with the defensive adaptations of skunks and bombardier beetles. The other hybrids tolerated his presence; usually from a distance. Today his unique gift proved invaluable as the noxious spray from his rectum blasted the unsuspecting guards. 'Smell this you morons!' he laughed as they doubled over in pain from the sulphur based chemicals.

The doors to Dr Cann's office buckled under the relentless blows raining down from the armour plated fists of an armadillo-gorilla hybrid. Dr Cann sat at his desk as the troop entered his room. They fanned out on either side of Marcus and Sebastian.

'Welcome back my children. How I've missed you all!' he smiled. 'Marcus my friend, and where's that boy of yours?' his narrow eyes scanning the group. 'Ahh...there you are my child. Come to me,' he said. Ike remained where he was.

'Really, you can't be angry with me. After all I only did what was best for you all.' He rose and walked around to the front of his desk, totally unafraid of the entourage.

'Enough Stephen, you lied to us all,' bellowed Marcus as he edged forward. Sebastian caught movement out of the corner of his eye. Three enormous insects emerged from behind pillars at the front of the room.

'Sphodromantis Viridis, commonly referred to as the African Mantis. These lovely females are larger and more aggressive than most other species.' He caressed the twitching head of the bright green hybrid adoringly. Marcus took a step back. 'These particular specimens are full body metamorphisms of navy seals. A gift from my friends in the military. Do you know that Dung beetles can pull over one thousand times their own body weight? A little something, I added for extra protection!'

'Why, Stephen? What do you want from us?' Marcus eyed the guards wearily. Stephen ignored the question.

'Those self-righteous fools at the Biotechnology Industry Organisation were swayed by public protests thereby outlawing full insect metamorphisms.' Dr Stephen looked genuinely hurt. 'Granted, the insect word is cold and brutal but so what. If something can be done, then it should be!' He slammed his fist into the desk causing his sentinels to become visibly excited.

This isn't going to end well, feared Sebastian.

Dr Stephen brushed both hands through his hair as he gained his composure. 'Anyway that's all irrelevant now.' He turned once again to face his adversaries. 'I should thank you Marcus. You've brought me everyone! This has turned out better than expected.'

'What are you on about?' asked Marcus calmly, now keeping a deliberate lid on this anger without taking his eyes of the insects. Marcus was part bear, but even he knew that he was no match for the mantis bodyguards.

'Sebastian was my gift to you. How else where you going to find your boy? I knew that only when you found him would you end your quest and come looking for revenge.' Sebastian recoiled from the revelation. 'Come now boy,' he addressed Sebastian directly. 'You can't be so naive as to think that this was all fate.'

Of course, realised Sebastian in a flash. *The opening in the fence plus a magnetron that could have easily returned the children automatically. All part of ingenious engineering!*

Marcus wasn't convinced. 'If what you say is true, why not just use a hybrid like Sebastian and capture Ike? Something doesn't add up.'

'True, very true my friend; but then as much as Ike with his gifts of camouflage, are valuable to me he fails in comparison to the goddess that you have hidden from me. Only you could lead her here.' He walked towards Celestra, flanked by his formidable guards, 'My darling child. I let you go too early. By the time we realised that your transformation was incomplete, it was too late. You were released. No matter, you are here now,' he nodded at one of his green companions, who immediately extended a frightening spiked raptorial foreleg behind Celestra, nudging her forward. She dared not refuse.

'Let her go you madman or else...!' The other mantis whirled around towards Marcus. A blow sent him reeling across the room.

'The best part about all of this my dear, is that you don't have the slightest inkling about how special you really are,' added Dr Stephen sympathetically. She was led away while Marcus and the others were held captive by the formidable Mantis guards.

Celestra was carefully wrapped in the membranous casing. She could hear Dr Cann clearly but was unable to respond. A viscous yellow fluid slowly filled the glass chamber holding her.

'Your unique ability to interrupt the genetic process and manipulate cell generation, is not accidental. Your serpentine form was the only base genome that allowed for a stable integration with the cells of Turritopsis Dohrnii commonly known as the immortal jellyfish. Man has been searching and experimenting with different types of tissues to discover the clue to immortality, but nature has already perfected this by millions of years of evolution.'

He peered into the chamber, touching the glass lightly with one hand. 'These jellyfish, have the ability to live forever by transforming or reverting to their primordial birth-stage after maturity. It is the only species in the whole world capable of transforming through cell transdifferentiation. Perhaps I should have not given up on you so easily my dear. You showed no signs of cellular longevity typical of perpetual cell regeneration. After all you, no your blood, to be more precise, holds the key to my salvation, my immortality! Through perpetual cell regeneration I will live on forever,' he clenched his fists and paced around the chamber impatiently.

'Ironic isn't it?' Dr Cann said almost with a ting of remorse. 'They say that the father lives on through the child. You gift me immortality but unfortunately my child you will not survive the extraction process.'

As consciousness tried to slip away from her, Celetra closed her eyes and visualised the tranquil waters of Sanguine Bay. Her breathing slowed and her mind calmed. A veil of serenity fell across her face as Stephen looked on. Her consciousness swirled in the land of dreams, oblivious to the physical world. Then, she focused.

Perhaps we may never know what happened that day but nature loves all of her children. The receivers of suffering and loss are sometimes rewarded with unexpected gifts. Divine intervention; Karmic fulfilment or biological anomaly: we may never know.

When Celestra opened her eyes, Dr Stephan Cann lay sprawled on the laboratory floor. His face drained of colour from suffocation. The membranous shell was torn and Celestra arose like a Goddess of the deep ocean. She walked out of the laboratory past more mantis guards, their triangular heads lowered almost as if in reverence to their new master.

Without speech she commanded the release of her comrades.

They all left Eden Towers that day and headed back to their domain. No one uttered a sound.

In the days that followed Celestra fulfilled the wishes of hybrids from near and far, gifting them their choice of being: human once again or human hybrid. Sebastian watched over her every evening as she swam out to sea, cleansing her mind and body of earthly concerns. Peace and love followed naturally for the pair who gifted the world with the first hybrid offspring. They would grow up naturally having never known any other way of life. All things come full circle.

The End

Adrift

Two unlikely companions
adrift in space make the most
remarkable discovery.

Adrift

The year 3089 saw the formation of the Intergalactic Alliance. After almost 300 years of territorial disputes and conflict, a welcome peace settled over the known galaxies. Joint expeditions and scientific exploration replaced wars and turmoil. The speed of joint collaboration was staggering and gave birth to a new quest, to find the truth about what lay beyond the known universe.

Brilliant minds, from diverse species, had all speculated about this. Zatheus from the deeply spiritual world of Utholea had theorised that the universe was eternal and ever expanding proportionally to the desires of all living entities. Alowlith, from the Sautune, showed with simple but eloquent equations that we lived in a 'Bubble Universe'. All known galaxies were encased within a bubble forming our universe which was part of other countless bubble universes. The most widely held belief was that there existed a great void beyond our known universe. In an attempt to put an end to all speculation, travelling beyond the known frontiers was inevitable. Transdimensional spacecrafts were created.

After almost 80 years of Earth time, the lazy but comfortable advance of the spacecraft came to a halt.

With a glassy silver exterior and tapered design resembling the deep-sea predators of the Misu water world, this remarkable voyager looked formidable. Presently it drifted aimlessly in space.

The almost inaudible humming of the control panel was interrupted by impatient beeps. White and purple lights flashed, illuminating the interior of the cabin, as the crystal control panel yawned to life. It had already passed through two dimensional warps as programmed by its creators, a group of likeminded intellectual beings from diverse civilizations.

These interludes between jumps were meant to recharge the crafts drives, using energy gathered from any neutron stars in the vicinity. Once fully charged it would automatically switch on and resume its mission.

The rude awakening triggered by a collision caused a status alert. The craft guarded its precious cargo as a mother might protect her unborn child. Despite the intricate programming and pioneering engineering, the creators believed that any discovery made by their artificially intelligent craft needed to be witnessed first-hand by the natural intelligence of a living being.

Jonathan was by no means the perfect pilot. However, his numerous years as a test pilot following an early retirement from Earth's elite Phoenix Avatars, added credibility to the mission. This all but overshadowed the insult to the intergalactic selection committee when only a handful of volunteers stepped forward for what many saw as a suicide mission. He did not care for glory or fame. When his wife Stephanie and daughter Jane were snatched from him by an accident, desire abandoned him.

La Nina as she was named by Jonathan was programmed to avoid collisions with astral bodies so it was rather illogical to the artificial brain of La Nina that such an event could occur. Like the Spanish ships of Earth's Age of Discovery that sailed the open seas, she was destined to ride across Nebulas that incubated infant stars.

In a determined effort to unravel this strange occurrence, La Nina's electronic brain processed zillions of probabilities, with fluid speed and accuracy; features contributed by the cyborg designers inhabiting the distant realm of Zeron. The hulking mass glided by, oblivious of the collision. Light from a nearby star gleamed of the Titan's outer covering. La Nina put herself into an orbit around the gigantic elliptical shape. Scanning the surface with alternating frequencies of sound waves, she attempted to formulate a picture of its composition.

The readings were inconclusive and once again illogical. If La Nina were capable of emotion, then alarming would be an understatement. Contained within this floating mass were traces of metal, organic matter and natural elements, some of which La Nina could not identify. This might explain why the object was undetected by the ships scanners resulting in a collision. La Nina was designed to detect all of these as separate bodies or with partial combinations but never with all of them interwoven into a single body.

The ship's audio scanners probed deeper using a lower frequency. La Nina's perfectly designed super logical brain struggled to comprehend the feedback. Emanating from this seemingly odd floating mass were signs of life!

The entire ellipsoid seemed to be alive. There were no signs of individual living entities within. Instead La Nina had awakened a floating giant!

Disturbed by the intrusive audio waves, the creature reacted defensively. Two long cylindrical protrusions grew out of one end of the creature. With flat disc shaped structures at the ends they resembled the antennae of some earth like insect. In an instant, La Nina experienced a malfunctioning of her primary circuits. The power surge emanated from the alien creature and La Nina had no defence.

Following standard emergency protocols, she initiated the subroutines that would gradually reverse the effects of the embryonic sleep chamber that carried Jonathan.

As consciousness flooded back to Jonathan, he was at first completely disorientated. Before his vision cleared he could feel the warm caress of the fluid encasing him. Dreamlike he opened his eyes and squinted with pain as he was bombarded with a kaleidoscope of colour.

Consciousness flooded in, displacing painful dreams of the Volasian battlefield. The translucent chamber opened releasing the artificially created embryonic fluid that filled his lungs and enclosed his body. He slumped to the floor naked and weak. Pain seared through his chest as he coughed up the fluid from his lungs.

It took a few seconds to register what had happened. Lightheaded he stumbled across to the crystal control panel and tried to verify the cause of the alert. La Nina would only awaken him if they had reached their goal or if there was an unforeseen emergency.

Outside in the cold of space, flocks of deep space Pez Diablo, resembling the manta rays of Earth's oceans but with three long undulating tails, glided by blissfully unaware of the drama unfolding. Their translucent bodies pulsating with a spectrum of light from within.

Despite his efforts Jonathan could not calm the frantic alerts erupting from the illuminated panel. La Nina could not be saved. His life support was dwindling by the minute. As he was on a mission to explore uncharted territory there was never any escape pod. Who would be there to rescue him? With the grit that came from many years in service, he dressed himself in his Colonel's uniform ignoring the pain from his until now inactive muscles. If he was going to die it would be a dignified death.

La Nina uttered her last electronic cry and then went silent. Jonathan lay against the cabin wall and closed his eyes as consciousness eluded him once again.

On the side of the space titan that faced La Nina there appeared an oval light blue glow on the giant's impenetrable shell. Jonathan disintegrated in a sparkling of light, just as La Nina broke apart and his body reformed within the blue sanctuary created by the giant.

As a boy, Jonathan would lie in his garden and enjoy the fragrant odour of the nearby pine trees and the drowsy fragrance of flowers that came on airy undulations. He breathed in those same fragrant odours now as he slowly regained consciousness. When his vision cleared he looked around at the hazy blue surroundings. The walls seemed to pulse with life as they gently expanded and contracted.

He rose to his feet and walked towards the entrance of the enclosure. It led to a passageway also filled with those wondrous fragrances from his childhood. The dimly lit passageway opened out to a larger chamber bathed in a strange luminescence. Jonathan could not fathom the source of this light. They seemed to emanate from the walls themselves. The chamber was lined with what appeared to be large wing backed seats sculptured out of the walls themselves. There were six of them, three on either side.

Relief swept over him as his mind latched onto the hope that he was rescued by a passing spaceship.

Cautiously he wandered further searching for the crew. Chamber after chamber, he roamed. All exactly the same. Each connected by a long passageway. After what seemed like hours, he stopped within another chamber that had no exit. 'Hello,' he shouted expectantly. There was no reply. Instead he detected faint vibrations running through the craft almost as if in response to his call. Jonathan succumbed to the bleak prospect that the craft was abandoned. Then how did he get here? Who had rescued him?

'I saved you, wanderer of the deep,' came the unexpected response.

Alarmed, Jonathan spun around, expecting to find his saviour. Instead there was no one, just the emptiness from before.

'You see what you see,' whispered a faint voice in his head.

Deep space explorers often reported hallucinations. Without a doubt he was having an episode.

'Believe, before you can see my child,' came the invisible but reassuring voice.

'Who are you?' he demanded.

'I am the seventh and last voyage craft of the Arora family. Conceived on the Centuri Off-world by the Viswa race, I am a sentient transport voyager.'

For eons there were rumours of living spacecrafts created by some magical and secretive civilization. They were believed to be so advanced that they could conceal their presence from even the most inquisitive detectors. Creations of a race that perceived themselves as observers of the known universe.

'Are you really a living spacecraft?' probed Jonathan unconvinced.

'If all possibilities are false then the impossible must be true.' Considering his predicament, Jonathan could not argue with that logic!

'Having come of wisdom now and served my creators well, I am free to wander as I please. In time I will join with all that exists. Energy flows and changes form and I too will blend harmoniously with the universe,' continued the philosophical and detached voice.

As improbable as it seemed, Jonathan accepted the astonishing truth that he was saved by a living craft that was now searching for its final bliss, death!

The cabin was illuminated by a fluorescent green light as a three dimensional hologram of a planet with three moons, rotated slowly on an invisible orbit just above his head.

'On Tiatune you may bide until your kin find you safe. The atmosphere will be welcome by your form. You will be safe.' Came the ancient voice.

Panic swelled up inside of him. Jonathan clung to calm despite his mind cringing with the thought of being stranded on some remote world. The planet had a name so that must mean it was either inhabited or visited for mining. Not all colonies were friendly to humans and he seriously doubted that this drifting titan knew or would even care about his predicament. Jonathan had never been a gambling man and he had no intention of taking up that venture now.

'Rest, for journeys end will be at hand with the passing of two moons of Shara.'

He could not fathom how long that would be but he had to find a way to persuade his saviour to abandon that idea before it ironically became the cause of his ruin.

Goliath, as Jonathan had named the space titan; partially to soften the reality that he was conversing with a machine, approached Tiatune. One wall of the cabin became transparent allowing Jonathan to see outside. The beige desert planet came into view. Rocks and other debris floated past as Goliath neared. There appeared to be five moons orbiting Tiatune! Jonathan reeled in disbelief as he recognised the orbiting moons as Onk warships. Their enormous size could easily allow them to be mistaken for moons. Onks had waged war with the United Space Council for generations and still refused to be part of the Intergalactic

Alliance. Their war strategy shrewdly employed destroying any orbiting moons of the poor planet that had fallen foul to their predatory appetite. This would spread fear through the hearts and minds of the inhabitants before the invasion began. Upon devouring the resources of the planet they would then move on in search of new worlds to conquer. Jonathan remembered with painful clarity the brutalities of war. He tried to bury the memories of what he had done under order of his commanders. The inhabitants of Tiatune were soon to discover the might of the Onks.

'We have to ...' he broke off in midsentence as Goliath changed course!

'Balance will be achieved. It always does. We cannot interfere.' Goliath, like its creators, would observe but never upset the delicate flow of creation.

Disbelief and desperation overwhelmed him.

'It will be a massacre, not a war if they don't have the technological knowledge to fight back!' raged Jonathan.

'I transport. That is all....'

The walls reverberated with the force of sudden impact. The decision had been made for them both. Like all living beings, Goliath was prone to folly and had underestimated the Onks capabilities. It could have cloaked itself into oblivion had it reacted sooner but was caught in the embrace of the deadly Hammer beam, as the Onks affectionately referred to their capture beam. Goliath was no ordinary ship, and with all the tenacity of a cornered Zelophyte, it broke free! Once again it reacted defensively but this time wisely chose to escape rather than fight. Common sense and self-preservation were powerful allies.

Baffled Onks were caught in its wake as Goliath entered trans-dimensional velocity. Jonathan was completely unprepared for this. He had always slept though La Nina's jumps. The walls of the chamber seemed to rush away from him. His body hovered in slow motion while his arms trailed residues of light. It was over almost as soon as it had begun.

Jonathan had a companion on this 'voyage of discovery'. Goliath too had a new experience, although of a somewhat distasteful nature. Escape was entirely new to Goliath. Without a predetermined trajectory and flight plan they had emerged on the other side of the jump into completely uncharted territory.

Once again, but this time in the company of Goliath, Jonathan was adrift. The interior of the cabin walls flashed with images of new worlds as Goliath tried feverishly to map out their surroundings. Jonathan pushed thoughts of Tiatune to the back of his mind as he focused on the present moment.

'No good. Seems hostile from the looks of all that volcanic activity. Nope that one too. Too much Zeonic radiation.' Jonathan eagerly offered his 'scientific expertise' as he shook his head disapprovingly. Goliath graciously accepted the help- although not needed. It somehow felt Jonathan's need to be involved. Amused, Goliath tried to remain serious. Jonathan was unaware that Goliath had adapted the interior displays so that he could decipher the data!

'Yes Sir! Glad to be of assistance. Now why don't we just take it nice and slow past that asteroid belt while I think of a way out of this mess.' suggested Jonathan with a serious and determined look. Goliath giggled.

'Hey! Seems like you have some minor turbulence there big fella. Better run a self-diagnostic.'

Goliath did not respond. Jonathan saw the reason for the sudden change. One of the displays took centre stage and rotated several times while all the others faded. The screen was empty. No planets were visible. Confused Jonathan looked closer. The sphere of swirling jumbled up light would be easier to see if you did not look directly at it. With an uneasy sense of awe and fear Jonathan recognised a black hole. They were already being draw towards the event horizon. Once they entered they would never be able to escape. Nothing, not even light could escape. Despite several attempts, even the bold cyborgs of Zeron failed to map out such strange anomalies.

Any other craft would have been caught in the chains of gravity from the black hole. Fortunately, Goliath was no ordinary craft. Engineered to live in the emptiness of space, it proceeded to avoid this uncharted realm.

Fear and excitement swelled up inside of Jonathan. Before them lay one of the mysteries of space. He could not remember a time when he was not acting under orders of one kind or another. Control by others had all but eroded his freedom and cost him fragments of his humanity. Here was a chance to redeem his sense of self-respect and worth.

'Would it not be splendid to glimpse the wonder that lies beyond the unknown? Before you blend with the universe, have an adventure. This is what it means to be alive. Not a life of servitude but a rejoicing in nature's creation!' said Jonathan.

'Yes, I would like to know the pleasure of discovery. I always wondered what my creators felt when they created us,' contemplated Goliath.

Neither of the voyagers knew if they would survive but they both knew that this was inevitable. As Goliath entered the black hole, time and space became irrelevant. Swirling light filled their vision. Fantastic, expanding and contracting crystal lattices followed, each competing with the other in a dance of vibrant colour. Then complete darkness! For what seemed an eternity, the two unlikely companions drifted in silence. Neither uttered a word. They could not judge distance so when they first saw the point of light, there was no telling how far away or how big it was. Perhaps, just a speck within reach or an enormity in the distance. However, there was no mistaking its growing intensity. The rapidly expanding light soon encompassed the two travellers. The glow was incredible. Goliath reduced the opacity of the screen in an attempt to shield Jonathan.

Goliath was drifting over pools of swirling blue and yellow masses separated by pure white space. Above remained the brilliant white light that stretched for eternity. As the pools below rushed by with increasing velocity, Goliath knew that they were accelerating.

'I am not in control,' whispered Goliath. Jonathan said nothing. Being alive, was relief enough for now. Then nothing. They came to a complete halt, as if they had not been moving at all. You might think that someone had pressed the pause button on a remote. The pull of momentum was absent much to the relief of Jonathan's insides.

The pools of swirling masses faded as the Entity came into view. As first it seemed to be just another point of light but the pulsating Entity was clearly not. There were several of them scattered around each hovering in their own space all around the fascinated travellers. As Jonathan gazed in awe, he saw far-sprinkled Entities tending systems. Wider and wider they spread, expanding, always expanding, outward and forever outward.

'Creations womb!' exclaimed Goliath, 'my Vishwa creators worshiped a Vortex of Creation. This must be the realm of creation. These must be their Gods. So this is where it all begins and ends,' exclaimed Goliath.

Feelings not words replaced understanding. Jonathan knew in an instant that the entities were creating worlds and galaxies for the pure joy of creation. They both realised intuitively that neither would have been able to enter this dimension without the other. A living craft cradling a tormented being. When he looked around again Goliath was gone. He was alone on his bed. Wonderful fragrances floated in from the open window. Time, our friend, had relaxed its grip on him.

'Daddy…daddy are you ready? It's time for our walk.'

Jonathan rose as the door opened.

The End

Aquatica

Amrit was known as the nectar of the Gods. It could cure any disease and prolong life.

Amrit was the most precious substance in all of the known universe.

Aquatica

'Know this to be the year of our Lord 5589. The last of the three worlds is about to be freed. Brute and mindless hordes, lost souls, roaming the oceans, will be blessed by the light of our knowledge and saved for all eternity.' Extract from a Shulgi priest's diary.

It all began with the discovery of Amrit, the substance known throughout the universe as the 'Nectar of the Gods'. Amrit could cure any disease. It could prolong life. Amrit was the most precious substance in all of the known universe. The ruling Emperor of the Universe, Emperor Harkin Brutus, sought to maintain absolute control over all Amrit production. Using the religious arm of the Empire, known as The Shulgi Sect, all new species discovered on new worlds were converted and subjugated. Amrit was found on only three worlds. Two of them had been mined until no Amrit remained. After years of frantic searching, Amrit was discovered once again, this time on the remote water-world of Asloria also known as Aquatica.

~

Thousands of years ago the sea reclaimed the land. Sweeping valleys and towering mountains succumbed to gigantic waves. The land animals breathed their last breath as Aquatica was born. The surface was an endless tranquil expanse in every direction where the clouds met the glassy surface on the horizon. At night Aquatica was a totally different world. Vicious hurricanes lashed the surface. Unimaginably powerful winds created mountains of angry waves.

From the coldness of space, Aquatica seemed a hostile and uninhabitable world, totally devoid of life. By chance or fate, an Imperial probe landed on the tranquil surface of Aquatica, one fateful day, revealing the planet's secret. Amrit was rediscovered. The merpeople inhibiting the ocean depths were converted by the Shulgi and served the Empire in mining the precious Amrit. Slaves to the Empire, they did not retaliate, but in their hearts, remembered the long held prophecy. A prophecy about a boy, a hero, who would lead them to true freedom.

Kraken drifted on the water's surface, completely disguised as an Elymus seaweed. It felt slightly disconcerting for him. Assuming the shape of lower life forms, altered the senses. However, this allowed him to remain camouflaged while his companions swam beneath him, searching for their elusive friend. For eight seasons, Kraken had won the Mespian run. Young Mermen were encouraged to race against each other across treacherous underwater terrain. Today, they raced just for the thrill of it.

At the opportune moment, Kraken changed into an Elodile. The streamline body and powerful tail of the predator, propelled him through the water as he descended towards the unsuspecting trio beneath. They were caught in his wake as Kraken torpedoed past them. The mermen were soon onto him and the chase resumed. Even at full speed, the mermen would never catch Kraken. Their smooth heads, with a single raised ridge running down along their backs, helped to steer their bodies as they swam. However, webbed hands and a single long tail were no match for one of the ocean's top predators. Kraken loved it! The thrill of the race was intoxicating. After what seemed like an eternity the mermen swam up alongside Kraken, who had slowed down for them. Kraken changed back into a merman. His friends knew of his special gift, a secret he shared with no one else, and certainly not during the Mespian Run. They gracefully accepted defeat, as only true friends would. The group changed course and headed deeper into the enchanting depths bordering the abyss. Here the ocean floor was decorated for miles in all directions, with bioluminescent plants and microscopic organisms. It felt like being in a different world. Here they could escape the realities of a life of servitude. Here they were free.

Colonies existed all over Aquatica, each housing a community of merpeople. Each colony was governed by a Lord who represented the will of the Emperor, and whose rule was absolute. Shulgi idols were placed within each settlement, close to the subterranean caves where the merpeople lived. Worship of these idols was compulsory. Merpeople were allowed to live a life of some normality, raising their families, whilst serving their Lords.

The Emperor Harkin Brutus was ruthless and cruel, as he was intelligent and cunning. For years he had languished under the crippling and agonising grip of Libitus disease. Grotesque sores covered his fragile body and exposure to light would cause the most excruciating pain. Only the life-giving Amrit could ease the pain and prolong his life. Lying in the darkened chamber he was attended by Shulgi priests. Over thousands of years the Shulgi had been ingesting, raw unrefined Amrit, causing their genetic mutation. Disproportionally large heads on dwarf-like bodies gave them an almost amusing appearance. This veiled a malevolent and twisted mind that harnessed a superior intellect. The Emperor yielded the Shulgi sect as a general might a weapon. It was the Shulgi that engineered the creation of colonial Lords from within native communities. By means of mind control, they appointed Lords. These new masters would not be foreign to the communities they ruled over and would have the advantage of knowing native customs and traditions. There were rumours of the Supreme High priest possessing Divine Sight and being able to see into the future.

Meanwhile, in another part of the galaxy, the fate of two smugglers was about to take an unexpected turn. The Avalt Raptor engaged hyper drive once it was clear of the asteroid belt. As the spacecraft accelerated, Takoda Knoi eased back on the controls, allowing the ship to run on autopilot. He was confident that it would outrun the Kyl space cruisers. Takoda was wanted in three different star systems for smuggling. This time he had managed, in his predictably charming manner, to infuriate the Kyl by failing to deliver the cargo on time. He relaxed into the pilot seat and cast a smug smile at his blue companion.

'Looks like we did it again mate! Told you-didn't I?' he boasted, 'No way those Kyl pilots can keep up with my baby.' Nurf nodded in agreement, a low whistling sound escaped his lips as he ran a final check on the life support systems.

'You bet buddy. Couldn't have said it better myself. The Kyl are far inferior,' said Takoda. It had taken him almost two years to understand the dialect of his shy blue skinned Murea companion. Nurf however, had come to understood Takoda within just a few days. The Murea were excellent mimics and wizards at navigating star charts. The perfect co-pilot! The Avalt Raptor came out of hyper drive, straight into the vicinity of an waiting Imperial squadron. An ambush!

'What on Jiomia! By the hairs of an Ocelot-Bison! I thought you said no one could track us!' exclaimed Takoda, his long plait of membranous hair rising with alarm. Nurf issued a defiant whistle in protest. *Guess the Kyl have friends in high places!* Thought Takoda.

The Avalt Raptor banked hard to one side as Nurf steered clear of the tractor beam coming out of the lead ship. Laser blasts flashed dangerously close to the ship's hull.

If they can't take us alive…guess they won't! A deafening blast reverberated through the ship. *We're hit!* A flying fragment struck Nerf unconscious. Takoda tried to adjust the ship's angle of entry as he steered it towards the nearest planet. *Get this wrong and we burn as bright as an Iris Butterfly!*

Back on Aquatica, Kraken and his companions were getting ready for harvesting. The Amrita plant from which the Amrit was extracted, grew beautiful blue flowers, containing the essence of the plant, Amrit. They grew in small groups, usually near submarine volcanoes. These underwater vents proved treacherous to navigate, even for Imperial underwater crafts. Mermen were tasked with retrieving the Amrita plants, while wearing only fragile bio-suits. However, the greatest threat came from the solitary predators of Aquatica's deep - the Megalodon. Even the powerful Imperial troopers had a deep and well-founded respect for these masters of the deep. Huge, almost as large as an Imperial cruiser, these twin tailed predators could wreak havoc.

In the Temple of Udur on the desert planet of Crecotera, the High Priests of the Shulgi gathered. For a hundred years there had not been such a gathering. Nine priests sat in a circle around the silver and gold dish. The colors of a thousand fragrances swirled in the unseen breeze of the heavily scented air. Their coloured smoke adding to the surreal atmosphere. The surface of the water within the dish rippled as the Priests focused upon their meditation. Within the murky depths of the liquid there appeared an animated image of Kraken with his friends swimming.

'*Su Ina Awil Tiamatu*,' they chanted in chorus (He be the man of the Abyss). The Supreme High Priest stared at the images as he listened to the chanting. *The union must not be realised,* he prayed.

Takoda released a Niopite bomb seconds before the Avalt Raptor could hit the water. *That should cover us,* he hoped. The radiation created by the blast would prevent the Imperial Ship's detectors from probing for any life forms and the metal fragments would be mistaken as wreckage. *No one's going to look for the dead!* The ship switched to aquatic mode. The composition of its outer shell changed into an almost liquid malleable gel. The Avalt Raptor could now adjust to the incredible pressures found at unimaginable depths. The craft became like the nature of water itself!

The group of mermen set off towards the harvesting fields. They had to pass over the Abyss to get to the nearest fertile Amrita site. The wide expanse over the infinite darkness that stretched deep into the depths of Asloria, was not easy to pass over. Strong currents threatened to drag unsuspecting victims into the Abyss. Merpeople feared the unknown depths where large forms moved. Kraken and his company of mermen passed over the beautiful bioluminescent fields bordering the Abyss. *Strange how something so beautiful would grow so near to something so feared*, though Kraken as he prepared to cross the Abyss with six of his working party. The Imperial guards did not need to accompany them. After years of Imperial rule, the Mermen were all too familiar with the consequences prescribed for not completing a task to their master's satisfaction or even worse- for trying to escape.

The Avalt Raptor moved through the water with incredible speed. At these speeds, supercavitation allowed for a reduction in friction by creating a bubble of gas around the Raptor, and combined with the semiliquid outer shell, allowed the craft to dive to incredible depths. Takoda was very proud of the Raptor. Nurf remained unconscious but Takoda had managed to move him into the medical unit, where he would soon be revived. As the craft descended, the Raptor's lights illuminated the darkness, revealing the rich and diverse world beneath the ocean waves. All manner of creatures moved about, both beautiful and terrifying. Takoda was about to search through the navigation charts before returning to check on Nurf, when the proximity sensors picked up a fast moving object approaching the Avalt Raptor. *150 knots! No creature could possibly travel so fast underwater. Must be an imperial sub- a pretty sleek one at that!* Thought Takoda.

He activated the ship's defences. The controls flashed red. *300 knots-impossible! Even the Raptor would struggle to achieve that!* A flashing blue dot on the screen showed that a collision was imminent. Takoda braced himself for impact. A tremendous explosion of silver-red fish swept over the Raptor. Sickening dull sounds told Takoda that some had crashed into the Avalt Raptor.

What kind of a world was this? Creatures like this are not supposed to exist. Panic and fear made breathing difficult. *At least we're still in one…* the shockwave threw Takoda off balance. *We're caught in their wake.* The Raptor was tossed about violently. It spiralled out of control. Takoda had to use all of his skill to steady the craft and regain control. *What next?*

They were about halfway across the abyss when Kraken stopped. Something was wrong! *Beklod, and they're heading this way!* It was too late; they would never make it. Kraken did not hesitate. His body pulsed and contorted, ripping the bio-suit, as he transformed into a Hukryl. The mermen grabbed onto the long tentacles as they we pulled swiftly to safety. Just before reaching the edge, Kraken stopped, and extended his tentacles forward as the last of his friends let go and swam over the edge of the Abyss to safety. Before crossing over himself, Kraken had to change back. The Hukryl body would be poisoned by the minuscule secretions of certain bioluminescent plants. Focusing his mind on the transformation, Kraken was completely unaware of the impending danger. A lone Beklod, travelling ahead of the others, slammed into his mermen body, knocking him senseless. Terror-stricken his friends watched helplessly as he fell into the deep, dark abyss. No one could get to him, as the school of Beklod passed between them like an underwater hurricane. The darkness reached out for Kraken, engulfing him.

The computer's on-board navigation module had over two hundred different star systems detailed. In addition to this Nurf had installed a state of the art planetary scanner that allowed the Avalt Raptor to 'see through' any planet. Readings indicated that a fissure in the planet's surface had created a 'doorway' through the planet. If they could pass through this opening, they would emerge on the other side of the planet safe from the Imperial forces that were surely following their last trajectory. Nurf was regaining consciousness just as Takoda engaged the autopilot.

'How do you feel buddy?' he said moving closer to Nurf. A faint whistle reassured Takoda that his trusty companion, although a little shaken, was going to be ok. 'We're not out of it yet! It won't take them long to figure out that the explosion was a smoke screen.' Nurf joined him at the controls as the Avalt Raptor gained momentum. They would have to pass through the planet, enduring incredible pressures. The unique shell of the Raptor would be able to adapt. Ahead they could discern the beautiful coloured bioluminescent landscape that boarded the abyss. The Avalt Raptor glided over the edge and descended into the dark depths below, before levelling out after a few hundred feet. The sensors on the control panel locked onto the descending body of Kraken.

'Mermen! By the hairs…I thought they were only a myth! So the stories are true.' panted Takoda as he pulled the unconscious body of Kraken into the Raptor through the small external hatch. The shimmering force field covering the opening, prevented the ocean from entering but allowed solid matter to pass through. The opening closed as Kraken passed through. Instinctively his body reacted to the absence of water and transformed into an Elymus seaweed! Kraken had regained consciousness.

Amazement doesn't quite cover it! It took a second or two for the information to sink in and then you could see the surprise register on their faces. Nurf let out a deafening squeal as he leapt into the open arms of Takoda, who stumbled backwards, mouth still open in shock! The commotion caused the equally surprised Kraken to assume the form of a terrifying spiked deep sea Maqul, with a mouthful of menacing sharp teeth. This time it was Takoda who screamed as Nurf just froze. Confused by his surroundings, Kraken moved between forms, finally settling on a remarkable replication of Takoda's body type. The comic duo passed out! When they awoke, they found themselves lying on the floor looking up into the face of a handsome young man. Kraken had touched Takoda a moment ago and allowed for an imprint to register a more accurate replication of a species that was clearly not native to Asloria.

'Look mister...or whatever you are. We meant you no harm!' pleaded Takoda.

Kraken tilted his head to one side as if trying to understand. Nurf was uncharacteristically silent. 'We just wanted to help.' Said Takoda. 'Are you going to eat us or something?' Nurf turned to Takoda. Murea people could not cry. Perhaps Nurf would be the first to do so!

An amused Kraken stepped back. 'Well, now that you mention it, I am feeling a little famished.' He looked at Nurf and smiled. Nurf cringed. 'I'm quite harmless I assure you. This is your vessel I take it?'

'You...you understand us?' exclaimed a bewilded Takoda.

'Of course I do, well this body does anyway.' Explained Kraken. 'Thank you for your help but I need to get back to my people. Can you help me?'

'No chance. We're being hunted down by Imperial soldiers and unless we get clear of this planet, well then, it's goodbye baby! If my history serves me correctly, then your people aren't much better off as slaves to the Empire. Seems to me that sticking with us is your best bet at this time. What do you say?'

Kraken was silent. He knew Takoda was right but in his heart, he longed to remain behind.

'First, we'll need to get you some clothes matey 'cause we aren't travelling across the galaxy with you like that!'

They descended into the depths, deeper than anyone on Asloria had ever been before. The lights probed the darkness, revealing creatures that you could not even imagine! At greater depths, they found the creatures living here had adapted to the immense pressure, by evolving more gelatinous body structures. Many also glowed brightly as their slim gelatinous bodies glided and danced through the water. Hours later, they emerged on the other side of the planet through a fissure in the ocean floor. The Avalt Raptor rose from the depths to break the surface of a stormy sea at night. Within minutes, it was on course for the Binary Quadrant, about 1500 light years away. Takoda's past as a smuggler, meant that he was familiar with outposts seldom visited by Imperial forces.

Planet Achadus, was the second planet out of twelve, orbiting around a red supergiant sun. Each of the other planets either sustained life naturally or were terraformed. The small planet, no larger than a moon, was home to Lord Alwyn, ruler of the Sholdi people. They were as beautiful as they were proud. Their external features were remarkably similar but the skin of every individual Sholdi was covered with rich hues of various colours, each as unique as a fingerprint.

All life on this world, had evolved to withstand the larger gravitational pull, exerted by this small, but dense planet. This in turn, resulted in a denser molecular structure for lifeforms, affording them incredible strength, when compared to most other species on different planets. Many Sholdi warriors were drafted into the elite and dreaded legions of the Emperor, The Rajshakti. They were the most feared and skillful warriors in the known universe, and it was the military might of these terrifying soldier-fanatics that kept the Imperial Throne safe for thousands of years.

In return for the use of his vast and strategically located trade routes, Lord Alwyn, was allowed a somewhat dubious immunity. Imperial troopers seldom visited these regions and the local civilizations were granted freedom of religion, much to the disapproval of the Shulgi. This agreement proved mutually beneficial and more profitable than war.

The Shulgi had bided their time with a fierce determination. The poison given to the Emperor, veiled as Amrit claimed its victim. Forgotten to many but still used by the Shulgi, the Universal Antidote, kept the Emperor alive by mimicking many of the healing and life sustaining properties of Amrit. The High Priest of the Shulgi took control of the Empire and sought brutal revenge upon the Mermen blamed for the ill refined Amrit. A new sovereign ruled the Empire, a sovereign hiding a deep and terrible fear.

When Lord Alwyn heard of the arrival of the Avalt Raptor, he summoned Takoda and Nurf at once. 'Good news travels fast!' he laughed as the trio entered the hall. 'So what brings you to Achadus my old friend? Not smuggling again are you?' asked Lord Alwyn as he leaned forward and feigned a look of discontent. 'You do remember that I have to keep the peace with the Empire?'

'Of course my Lord. Just visiting some old friends. You know how I love your beautiful planet! Just can't stay away.' Lord Alwyn looked unconvinced. He turned to Kraken. 'And who is this?

'Kraken, of the Merpeople of Asloria!' came the proud reply. All eyes turned to Kraken, who stood alongside Takoda and Nurf, tall and muscular in his Sholdi body. Princess Sheera stepped forward. 'A merman shapeshifter! Astonishing,' she said, 'The shapeshifter gene is the erratic and inexplicable gift of our universe, bestowed upon a chosen few. Yet here you are, exhibiting and parading yourself with little respect for the mystical power afforded to you.' Even Lord Alwyn, was startled by his daughter's audacious remarks.

Before Kraken could reply, Lord Alwyn intervened. 'I do apologise. My daughter offers you no insult. Princess Sheera speaks her mind as all nobles should. In fact, while you are my guests, it would be an honour for the princess to show you around our beautiful home.' Princess Sheera cast a fiery gaze at her father. Kraken smirked.

The Sholdi too had a prophecy. It had been foretold by the Council Elders generations ago, when the Great Book of Odrus was consulted. A union between a Sholdi princess and an offworlder would lead to the birth of a new age for their people. Lord Alwyn could not explain why he took such a liking to Kraken, but his kindness would change Sholdi history forever.

The Supreme High Priest of the Shulgi was unrelenting in his determination to find Kraken. Mercenaries were dispatched to the furthest reaches of the Galaxy to seek out the boy. Lord Alwyn protected the fugitives. Takoda and Nurf were to remain in hiding while Kraken was sent to the Rune Nexus, a collection of thirteen planets serving as the training bases of the Sholdi army. Here Sholdi soldiers were trained in all manner of martial arts. Kraken excelled in combat. He could adapt to and exploit any of the varied and inhospitable environments that were meant to test the resolve of the proud Sholdi warriors.

However, nothing could remain hidden from the Shulgi for long. Lord Alwyn's treason was repaid with Sholdi blood. Planet Achadus was almost completely ruined in the war that ensued. Just before the final assault, Lord Alwyn entrusted

Takoda and Nurf with the safety of the princess. The Avalt Raptor, outmanoeuvred the Imperial cruisers and carried the Princess to safety. Kraken met them on one of the many obscure outposts that Takoda had visited in the past. With heavy hearts, the survivors embraced their destiny, as the Avalt Raptor carried them through what felt like a hopelessly dark universe.

Sheera knew of only one place where they might find refuge - on the wind swept world of Trone. A planet of stark contrast; where desert plains bordered immense grasslands surrounding lakes. Here her uncle Doran lived in seclusion. Once known as Doran the Unconquerable, on account of his unyielding ferociousness in battle, he had helped the Sholdi army gain victory against the Kyl during the three years of territorial disputes for the Rune Nexus. Doran had no love for the Empire and when his brother Lord Alwyn, entered into that dubious partnership with the Empire, the headstrong Doran left.

The wind howled like a beast, as it tore against the door of the subterranean shelter that was home to Doran. News of his brother's death hurt him deeply despite the rift that had grown between them. Overwhelmed with remorse,

Doran sheltered and provided for his niece and her companions. He relocated them to a retreat on the edge of an enormous lake, mindful that Kraken would need to revert to his merman form occasionally. In the days that followed, Takoda and Nurf left the safety of Trone, for great lengths of time, to meet with members of a small but passionate resistance that had been formed.

Sheera and Kraken grew closer to each other. Once worlds apart, they now revolved around each other, drawn together by an understanding of each other's pain. A child, a boy, was born to them. Doran named him Karna.

Karna was born with all the powers of his parents combined. His little body was immensely strong and beautiful like that of his mother's while also possessing the shapeshifting ability of his father. Embedded within his genetic coding were the 'biological memories' of all life forms that his father had encountered, so Karna could transform into any of these at will. Pity for his parents, who sometimes had to deal with the tantrums of an infant who could hurl boulders or transform into all manner of beasts! Uncle Nurf, as Takoda liked to call him, was fond of bringing the little Karna gifts whenever he returned home. Joy and apprehension were mixed together whenever he presented them for no one could predict the outcome. Get it right and you receive hugs and kisses that felt like blows from a hammer. Get it wrong and you better disappear - fast! Fortunately, the cunning teamwork of his parents, prevented him from harming himself or others. But there was one more entirely unique talent that Karna possessed - the voice. He could command both men and beasts using the voice. It was rumoured that some Shulgi priests, who were severely mutated, could generate the voice. Doran took it upon himself to train and discipline the boy. As he grew, and even from a young age, Karna demonstrated uncanny skill at combat. Doran instructed the young warrior in the Sholdi deadly arts, many that he had never shared with the Sholdi army, fearing that they would be stolen by the Empire when some Sholdi were recruited into their ranks.

The Empire eventually discovered where the family was hiding. They sent their deadliest assassin. The craft landed on a desolate, dry, sandy plain, some distance from the cabin. Stealth mode engaged, it was completely invisible. Within seconds the assassin was speeding along on a flying cruiser, headed for his prey. His orders were clear, capture the child- kill anyone who interferes.

Sheera and Kraken were out training. They would not return until much later that evening. Doran and Karna spent time at home. The assassin padded without noise around the outside of the cabin. His people, the Nekojin or cat-people, were notorious assassins. As if made of the darkness itself, he entered their home. Doran was completely unaware of the intruder. The dart pierced his skin, releasing the neurotoxin. The poison travelled through his body, faster than the nerve conduction velocity. Doran was dead before he even felt the dart. Karna was asleep and would remain so thanks to the drug administered into his little body. *Mission accomplished.*

They found Doran sprawled on the floor, dead. Karna was gone. Sheera and Kraken, said nothing. Fear washed over them, threatening to suffocate them. Suddenly Kraken exploded into violent motion. Taking the form of the sleek and swift desert raptors, Kraken went after his son and his captor. Sheera followed some distance behind. Kraken caught up with the Nekojin just as he disembarked from the cruiser with Karna. His lungs burned as if they were filled with acid. He would not be able to hold this form for long. He needed water.

Without stopping, Kraken launched himself into the air and executed a somersault in one fluid motion that brought him bearing down onto his enemy. The Nekojin swivelled in his direction. Agile and lethal, the cat-assassin evaded the charging Kraken. From within his robe, he withdrew a short staff that could yield several different configurations of bladed weapons, the preferred kill-blade of assassins. Evading the attack, he simultaneously brought up the weapon directly into the charging Kraken, cutting him deeply on his forelimb. The poisoned blade had a lethal touch.

However, Kraken was not so easily overcome. As he crashed into the ground he partially transformed his forelimbs, discharging dozens of sharp quills that went whizzing through the air. Instinctively the cat-assassin blocked with a shield configuration as the quills clanged into the metal. Kraken was weakening with every motion, the poison draining his strength. The Nekojin raised his blade, intending to deliver the fatal strike. The blade mummed a low, swift sound as it descended. Kraken looked up. In that frozen instant before impact he saw Sheera.

The blow sent the stunned assassin flying. He shrieked as his ribs were disintegrated by the kick. Gold-yellow blood escaped his lips as he tried to raise to his feet. Two more blows from her ended his pain forever. She turned to Kraken. 'We have to leave this place.' he moaned, 'It's not safe anymore. Don't worry about me...uh, my body will adapt to the poison as well. Call Takoda.'

Years passed. They roamed the galaxy, never staying in any one pace for too long. Takoda and Nurf stayed with them. The young Karna grew up strong and able. His parents tried to ignore the inevitable truth, but Karna questioned everything. They both knew that returning to Asloria, was destined.

In the year of 'endless storms', when the calm of the day gave way to turbulent storms, typical of the tempestuous nights, they returned to Asloria. The vast ocean planet afforded them many sanctuaries. The new regime had been persecuting the mermen. Hope was now only a dream for them. The Empire cared only that Amrit production was at its peak. If Karna was to liberate his people, as foretold by the prophecy, then he would have to unite the subjugated and broken mermen. The prophecy stated that the true hero would be able to assert his right to rule if he could conquer an age old nemesis, the Megalodon.

Without weapons or defences of any kind, Karna confronted the Titan of the deep. Blood would draw it out from the dark depths where it roamed. Karna bit into his own hand and allowed a little blood to escape- then he waited. The invitation to battle had been sent. Moments dissolved into hours before it appeared. Out of the inky blackness, Karna could discern the outline of the approaching monster. The slow movement belied the speed that it was capable of. Razor sharp teeth adorned its mouth. The Megalodon was out to kill. The irresistible lure of blood made it mad. In the battle that ensued between predator and prey, no quarter was given. Karna changed between forms with fluid movements, attacking and evading constantly. He did not wish to kill the beast, just weaken it. When he felt that the moment was right, he issued a sonic blast using the voice. Weakened and tired, the Megalodon yielded to the will of its master.

With the help of Takoda and Nurf, Karna launched the first in a series of guerrilla attacks against the Empire soldiers. Takoda had enlisted the help of a small but lethal group of rebel fighters. The varied ensemble of fighters followed Karna across Asloria, launching random and fleeting attacks with the intention of liberating his people and crippling Amrit production. All eyes turned to Asloria. In a desperate attempt to ensure the continued production of Amrit, without which the Sholgi priests could not survive, the Rajshakti were summoned by the Empire.

Bloody underwater battles ensued in which many rebel fighters died. Empire technology coupled with the ferociousness of the Rajshakti, saw hope dwindle away. Karna would not give up! Riding his Megalodon, he travelled across Asloria gathering his kin to him. The reclusive Dolphipus tribes of the Eastern seas and the immensely strong Lazu tribes of the Northern seas came. Using the voice, Karna gathered an army of Megalodon. These enormous creatures, smashed through the Rajshakti ranks and created havoc. Many of them were sacrificed in this way but afforded Kraken and his army a strategic advantage. Karna launched a decisive attack against the Rajshakti twenty-two days after the first attack.

The Shulgi High Council had to come to terms with Karna. He was to be allowed an audience with the Supreme High Priest of the Shulgi. The gigantic golden metal sphere floated in the skies of Crecotera miles away from the sacred Temple of Udur. Glittering in the sunlight, its polished surface, impossibly smooth. Encased within the protective golden outer shell, was a city of unrivalled beauty and splendour. Gold and jewels from all corners of the Empire were used to adorn the inner walls. The opulence of the city was a symbol of the Empires' might. Within this enchanting floating city, Karna and his closest companions were brought before the Supreme High Priest.

Seated upon cushions within a glass sphere, that floated just above the floor, was the Supreme High Priest. The sphere glided in gently, surrounded on either side by formidable Rajshakti warriors. With their long flowing red capes and fighting staffs in hand, they looked magnificent and deadly at the same time. Even though their faces were masked by armour, Nurf and Takoda could feel their piercing stare. Leading this procession were a group of Shulgi priests. They moved slowly, too slowly, as they chanted sacred mantras, nodding their deformed heads that were hidden within hooded robes.

Thin, almost reptilian in appearance, the priest surveyed the audience with narrow warmongering eyes. A smooth, youthful complexion concealed his true age which had been prolonged by Amrit. His gaze fell immediately upon Karna- the Hero. A spark- who would lead, sacrifice and inspire; lighting a fire in the hearts of his people. The High priest hated him with a dark and fierce anger. Karna stood magnificent like a demi-god. Tall, muscular and radiant with interlacing hues of colour displayed proudly on his Sholdi skin. His four arms replicated after a touch from his Asura rebel fighters.

The High priest spoke, 'You are charged with high treason young Karna so you ...'

'This is not a hearing!' interrupted Kraken.

'Silence!' The universal translator relayed the command with crystal clarity. 'I will decide what is just. You have broken a long held peace for which you will pay the supreme penalty,' declared the priest, his eyes never leaving Karna.

'There is a kind of peace that can only be found on the other side of war,' Karna smiled as he spoke the words.

'What insolence! Perhaps you need a lesson in manners first my young upstart. Let's see you smile now. Bring in the beast,' he ordered.

The monster was a predator. Its huge muscular frame moved with remarkable stealth as it circled Karna. The wolf like head had a mouth lined with long teeth, serrated like a knife. Its body, however was covered in what looked like scales. The beast seemed to choose its shape after assessing Karna. The scales began to vibrate and emitted a low pitched sound as they changed colour. In the blink of an eye, it changed into a massive towering beast taller than Karna. Two huge arms covered with poisonous suckers and ending in sharp curved talons, grew out of the side to the beast. Karna did not move.

'He was once like you, a shape-shifter. Oh, yes! Full of himself, proud of his unique gift. We taught him obedience all right,' mocked the High Priest.

For seven long years on Crecotera, they had tortured him. Physical and mental agony the likes of which no creature should endure. Finally, broken, he remembered nothing of his former self- he had become their beast. In an instant it was upon Karna. Moving faster than the eye could see, it lashed out at him, tearing Karna's flesh. Karna responded with a hammer-fist to the side of the beast's head, sending it reeling backwards. Before it could recover, Karna pounced on it. The battle was a sight to behold! Two adversaries, equally matched. Changing shapes embracing each other in a deadly dance. Talons clawed against scales, fists struggled against tentacles. In the final moments, when it seemed as if neither would emerge victorious, Karna seized his chance. He had the beast pinned to the floor. Rancid saliva mixed with blood, dripped from its mouth as Karna pressed down on it. Karna used the voice as a weapon. The sound went deep into the beast's brain, deep into its soul. It locked eyes with Karna in that final moment as life escaped it. Peace, it had found release.

Karna rose to his feet turning to face the High Priest. Stunned silence. Then suddenly all those assembled spoke with a single voice, 'He is the one, the one to set us free.'

Karna had fulfilled the prophecy. Where there was oppression he brought freedom; where there was darkness- light. A royal marriage to the Princess Sheera on Planet Achadus, saw a new dawn for the Sholdi people. The Sholdi kingdom was restored to its former glory. The once persecuted and scattered mermen were united and protected under their new ruler. To the Shulgi, Karna offered forgiveness and a chance at redemption, for only the truly strong could forgive.

'We drink the Amrit to extend our lives, to extend our minds. The nectar of the gods, cleanses our hearts of desire, for we seek only to serve our new master. We are blessed by the light of his grace and saved for all eternity.' Extract from a Shulgi priest's diary.

On Asloria, tranquillity returned to the turbulent seas.

The End

Also by the same author:

Maths

through

Story and Rhyme:

A Revision Guide for Key Stages 3 and 4

ISBN: 978-0955892004

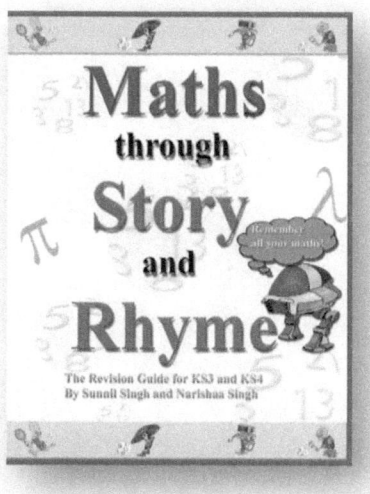

Available from Amazon and other leading wholesalers.